GATHER TOGETHER
IN MY NAME

GATHER TOGETHER IN MY NAME

TRACY PRICE-THOMPSON

ATRIA BOOKS

New York London Toronto Sydney

ATRIA BOOKS

A Division of Simon & Schuster, Inc.
1230 Avenue of the Americas
New York, NY 10020

First Atria Books trade paperback edition May 2008

ATRIA BOOKS and colophon are trademarks
of Simon & Schuster, Inc.

For information about special discounts for bulk purchases,
please contact Simon & Schuster Special Sales at
1-800-456-6798 or business@simonandschuster.com.

Designed by Suet Y. Chong

Manufactured in the United States of America

10 9 8 7 6 5 4 3 2 1

Library of Congress Cataloging-in-Publication Data
Price-Thompson, Tracy, 1963–
Gather together in my name : a novel / by Tracy Price-Thompson.—
1st Atria Books trade pbk. ed.
p. cm

ISBN-13: 978-1-4165-3304-7 (trade pbk: alk. paper)
ISBN-10:   1-4165-3304-4 (trade pbk: alk. paper)

1. Death row inmates—Fiction. 2. African American men—Fiction.
3. Rapists—Fiction. 4. Children—Crimes against—Fiction.
5. Murders—Fiction. I. Title.
PS3616.R53G38   2008
813'.6—dc22   2008008643

This work is dedicated to the memory of Mel Taylor, acclaimed author of *The Mitt Man*

September 23, 1939–July 30, 2007

They say God brings people together for a reason, and when we've been blessed with the gift of a beautiful relationship we want the world to know it.

Mel Taylor was my friend. We met on the internet after his novel *The Mitt Man* was published to acclaimed reviews, and I was delighted to get my hands on a copy. Mel contacted me sometime after that, and the first time I heard his voice I knew he was something special. Mel embodied the spirit of a warrior man, someone self-assured, highly intelligent, and fiercely in love with life, knowledge, and the written word.

Over the years Mel and I developed a relationship that was unlike any I've ever experienced. Many writers claim to support and uplift other authors, but Mel truly did. We talked all the time. About life, death, successes, failures, books, our families, and the love of writing that we shared. Mel quickly became a very important part of my life, and everyone in my family, from my husband down to my youngest child, understood and respected the bond that Mel and I shared.

I looked up to Mel. He was my elder and I respected his wisdom, his colorful and sometimes harrowing life experiences, and his tried and tested judgment. There were many days when I turned to him in a time of family crisis or personal chaos, and always Mel was there for me, as if I were his only friend, and the counsel and guidance he gave me was sometimes the only thing that stood between me and a mistake. Between me and uncertainty. Between me and failure. I relied upon him. I leaned on him and he held me up. I cried to him and he gave me comfort.

Many readers and authors knew Mel in his physical state. But I never laid eyes on him. We never physically met. He was my good, good friend for years, yet I've never seen him, or touched his hand, or hugged his shoulder, or had the pleasure of watching him smile.

I knew Mel only through his voice and through his heart. He was my confidant, my mentor, and my voice of reason. We cherished each other from the distance of a keyboard and a telephone line, yet Mel built a relationship with me that was primary in my life and will always live in my heart.

The conceptualization of *Gather Together in My Name* was, like many of my works, a collaborative process with Mel Taylor. Mel was very open about his past; and having spent time in the penitentiary, he'd gained a thorough understanding of the ills of the American justice system as it relates to the race of the victim and the race of the accused. Mel baby-stepped me through each word of this novel. He fed my muse with his bare hands. He helped give form and depth to the character Shyne Blackwood, and was an invaluable source of insight and creativity.

Mel was good to me. Better than a friend. Better than he had any reason to be. Over the years he gave me so much life and literary fortification that I'll never have to go without. I can only hope that during the course of our friendship I gave Mel something of value as well, and I will love him and keep him in my heart until the day we finally meet . . . for the very first time.

ACKNOWLEDGMENTS

To my husband, Greg, thank you for understanding the worth of a woman and for personifying the truest measure of a man. (D!GWTHDOMM!) Because of your love and high character, our lives are peaceful, grounded, without pettiness or envy, and we are thereby able to fully share our blessings and talents with others.

To Ken Atchity and Emily Bestler, thank you for your support and encouragement on all levels, and for allowing me the creative freedom to tell the diverse stories granted by my muse. It's both a pleasure and an honor to be on the same team with the two of you. Your input in helping to shape my stories is appreciated and invaluable, and I could not have accomplished this work without either of you.

To my sister, Michelle Nixon; my dear friends Carmelia Scott-Skillern, Linda King, Robin Oliver, Deborah Woodley, Stephanie Howard, Edie Hall, Relisa Wilson,

Acknowledgments

Sherrell Pippens, Barbara Jackson, and Shawn Bell for your love and support of my work.

To my sister-readers, Rubina Collier, Stephanie Pickett, Annette Thomas, Linda Mitchell, Barbara Mitchell, Sandra Simms, Cindy Abernathy, Yolanda Richardson, and Florence Moore, thanks for sharing your love of good literature and good times!

To Marisa Moore, Antira Albea, Regina Williams, Dr. Denyse Ray, and Ursula Sellers, thank you for your belief in Sister4Sister Empower Ourselves, and for your hard work on behalf of the organization. It is sisters like you who help young ladies of color reach their potential and soar to their greatest heights. You powerful, phenomenal ladies truly embody the S4S motto: "Want for Your Sister What You Want for Yourself."

Peace and balance, Tracy.

GATHER TOGETHER
IN MY NAME

OCTOBER 12, 2007

THE DEATH HOUSE

SHYNE "Sing," I whispered into her hair as I squeezed her hips and pulled her deeper into my arms. An old jam was playing, some smooth cut by Mint Condition. I moved her across the floor, half-fucking her as we slow-danced in the heat. I was big, black, and bursting with juice as I cupped her ass and grinded along with the bass boom of the music. She teased me back, and my wood nearly cut a hole in my pants as I humped her midsection, trying to stick her right through her clothes.

She sang softly, the words to the song muffled against my

neck as she sucked and nuzzled, doing her best to raise a purple hickey on my midnight skin.

"Stop, Shyne," she laughed as I slapped her big bottom, then moaned as it jiggled in the palm of my hand. I buried my face in her hair, excited by its scent and its coarseness, knowing the strands between her legs would be softer and oh so slick, if I could just get past some of these damn clothes.

She was a tall girl. Damn near tall as me, and her breasts were like warm chocolate mountains under my lips. Chocolate mountains with a cherry on top. My mouth watered and she sucked in air as I bit down on them, teasing their peaks as my body jerked with need. I slid my hand up her bare thigh and felt steam. I lifted her skirt and dug between her legs, a sweet, tangy moisture coating my fingertips as I searched for her slit.

"Gimme some pussy," I demanded, my voice husky and desperate as I struggled to get up in her. "Come on, open up them damn legs."

"They are open," Deborah whispered sweetly. "You just can't get between 'em, Shyne." Her lipstick was blood-red as she laughed in my face. "You got fried, remember? You fucked that little white girl, Shyne. Now your black ass is dead."

I sat up in the darkness, drenched in sweat and gripping myself.

I was rock hard and throbbing as I squeezed my wood through the thin blanket clenched in my hand. My eyes darted around the small cell and I forced myself to calm down as real life settled in around me. Those weren't no sexy clothes I was fighting to penetrate, just a musty prison blanket. There was no Deborah licking my earlobe and dancing and quivering all over my fingers neither. Just another lustful jailhouse dream in the darkness of night.

In the darkness of my *last* night.

Let me just keep it funky for you.

I'm a street niggah, a hustler, a certified gangster. Almost everything you heard about me is true. I got drunk and got high too. I robbed and stole, and yeah, I've even killed. I've been locked up and locked down. I've knocked a couple of birds on their asses and put a look in my mama's eyes that would make you crawl on your knees in shame. I've always been the kind to take what I wanted, and truth be told, they could've put me down a long time ago. If not for this, then for something else. Armed robbery, drug trafficking, money laundering . . . they don't send you to the penitentiary for being no choir boy. I was a criminal then, and I'm a criminal now. The streets are hungry and I've always paid my dues.

Difference is, this time I gotta pay with my life.

• • •

She was only three, Terrie's little girl. She was a skinny little kid with blond hair and blue eyes, just like her mother.
Me and Terrie had us a little sex thing going back in the
day, right after I walked out on my girl Deborah and
before Terrie's kid was born. She'd hooked up with some
white guy in college who introduced her to crack and ice,
and her family had disowned her. They took her back in
when he got her pregnant, though, and helped her get up
on her feet. Me and Terrie hadn't been together in a real
long time, but she was still feeling me and would always
offer me a little bit of head whenever we crossed paths.

I ain't gonna lie. I'd be tempted sometimes, but I
was back with Deborah again by then, and just thinking
about what would happen if her crazy ass found out was
enough to make me laugh and keep my pants zipped.
Terrie's game was cool and all, but she wasn't worth
going through no drama with Deborah. Plus, her family
wasn't feeling black people like that, and dealing with
them got to be more trouble than one skinny white girl
was worth. But Mama really liked Terrie. She had a thing
for the girl, so even after we broke up Terrie still came
around the house from time to time.

While I was busy living the street life and stacking
my rap sheet, my brother Shug had gone to college and
then on to law school, leaving the hood behind and

moving up in the world. He was a six-figgy-niggy, a rising politician, a mover and a shaker, a black man with a bank account. Shug rested in a sweet four-thousand-square-foot crib with a wide green lawn and marble floors. A Benz was parked in his driveway and a Beemer chilled in his garage. His crib was his hard-earned castle, and he lived just like a king up in there too. When we were kids Shug had his sights set on becoming the second black mayor of New York City, but shit, I told him why stop there. As far as I was concerned he could've taken it all the way to the White House.

You know a black man in Shug's line of work had to project a certain image, and my brother wasn't shy about draping good money across his back. With two walk-in closets full of tailored suits, another one stacked with designer shoes, and a handful of genuine Rolexes, my brother was living the black man's dream. He had a barber from around the way who edged him up every other day, and a young Asian chick came to the house and gave him one of them sissy-ass facials once a week. Man, Shug Blackwood stepped outta his front door in French or Italian suits damn near every day, looking like a white-people–user-friendly nonthreatening successful black buppie on the rise.

But I knew him. I knew him better than anybody, and

underneath the shine my brother was just as hood as he could be. He mighta rubbed elbows with powerful white folks from dawn to dusk, but Shug was a G. He knew the streets and stayed connected to his people, and you had to respect that. So when Shug said he was throwing an old school barbeque for Mama's birthday, the whole hood was down.

All our boys from around the old way had shown up, and Mama had insisted on inviting Terrie and her daughter, but my girl Deborah was there too. Tripping. She just couldn't get past the fact that when I walked out on her I had actually messed with a white girl.

"I don't know *what* the hell you was thinking, messing with one of those nasty bitches, but I ain't playing with you, Shyne," Deborah had warned me. "Let me catch your black ass anywhere near that dirty crack ho and I'ma drag you *and* her around by her stringy-ass hair."

"I already told you. Terrie's cool. Her and Ben are having another baby so she don't even smoke no more. The only reason she came is because Mama invited her. Ain't nothing happening between us."

On the real, Mama was the one Deborah had a problem with, not Terrie. It burned my baby up to watch Mama sit around laughing and grinning all over a white girl, when she didn't have two good words to say about Deborah's bomb body and pretty brown face.

Deborah had walked around Shug's crib with her fine ass on her shoulders all day, but I got out there in that big backyard and had me a good time. A bunch of our old neighbors from the projects had come out to see Shug's new house and it was like being with family. The music was hot. Everybody ate and danced, you know how we do. We played a little bones, a few hands of Tonk. Talked some real loud bullshit over a tight game of Whist.

Shug had the beer and liquor flowing in the backyard and folks were getting nice, but I kept ducking inside the crib to hit his private stash 'cause Mama had already got on my case about drinking the day before.

"Don't you go around your brother's house acting stupid tomorrow, you hear? Shug done built himself a good name in this city and everybody knows how you like to black out and lose your mind when you drink. My baby can't afford to be mixed up in none of your mess, Shyne, so you better stick to orange juice if you know like I do. I ain't having no foolishness outta you, boy. You hear me? There ain't no excuse for it and I mean it."

I wasn't trying to hear that shit from her. I mean, I can't say Mama didn't have a reason to fuss, but I didn't go for her telling me what to do, and I didn't need her throwing my past up in my face like that either. Yeah, liquor did me bad, and that was a well-known fact. I just couldn't hold it. It got me loose, and whatever monsters I managed to keep muzzled down when I was sober sure as hell came out of me juiced.

Well I fixed Mama's ass. I drank like hell that night 'cause I'm a grown-ass man and I can get just as loose as I want. Hell, *everybody* was drinking and cutting up. But then Deborah and Terrie got to acting stupid and making all kinds of noise, and when Mama jumped in and started screaming on my girl, my liquor told me to jump in and get loose on Mama too.

Man, I wrecked shit up in Shug's crib. I only remember bits and flashes, but I heard all about it the next day. I do remember Terrie getting up in my face, making me toss her ass across the room. Mama had started yelling and telling Shug to put me out before his neighbors called the cops and got him in trouble, but none of that noise meant a damn thing to me. At some point I must have blacked out, and I was still in a fog when Deborah woke me up the next afternoon.

"Shyne!"

She had dragged me home with her, crazy-drunk and out of my mind.

"Get up, Shyne!"

My head was bamming and I was sprawled out across her bed. I opened one eye and glared at her as she stood over me, then rolled over onto a plate of gnawed-down chicken bones that were on the bed beside me. I licked my lips, and the burn of Tabasco sauce hit me and I groaned.

"Somebody killed Terrie last night! I just saw her boyfriend, Ben, crying on the news!" Deborah covered her mouth, her pretty brown eyes shocked wide. "Damn . . . this shit is crazy! I can't believe it! I was just about to beat her ass at Shug's last night and now she's dead!" She shook her head quickly, then crossed her arms and squeezed herself tight. "Oh my God . . . that poor chick must have really suffered! It's all over the news. Somebody broke in through her window and stomped the hell outta her, then cut her throat. Whoever did it snatched Ari up too. Did you hear what I just said, Shyne? Terrie is dead, and her baby is gone!"

CNN was on it like white on rice.

First there was the Amber Alert. Then the ground search. Sympathetic white folks beat back bushes and crawled around in back alleys trying to find her. And two days later they did. In the basement of an abandoned building, deep in the hood, far away from the apartment Terrie's father had rented for them out in Westchester.

Little Arielle was all busted up. Raped. Strangled. Brutalized. The public was on edge. A baby killer was officially on the loose, and the media yeasted the fear factor up as high as they could get it. The next few days dragged by. Front doors were double-bolted all over Brooklyn, and little kids slept under the watchful eyes of their protective parents.

But I gotta give it to the NYPD. They knew their shit, and forensics is a bad motherfucker. They ran some tests, put together a list of suspects, and the next thing I knew they came gunning for me like I was Osama bin Laden.

"You're under arrest for the murder of Terrie Mills, and the rape and murder of Arielle Mills!"

They bum-rushed me inside Mama's house, and you shoulda seen her face when they pushed past her and kicked down the bedroom door.

Rape? Murder? What the fuck?!

I denied that shit at the top of my lungs but the cops cracked me in the head anyway and it was on. I fought so hard it took six of them to cuff me and drag me outta that house, but it was Mama who really hurt me. When they told her what I was being arrested for she hit me with a look so cold that it was her eyes, and not those billy clubs, that finally put me down on the ground.

Man, I looked like public enemy number one in my bright orange jumpsuit. They ran my mug shot on the front page of the paper, side by side with Terrie and her little girl, and next to all that blond hair, and those blue eyes and ringlet curls, I looked bigger and blacker and meaner than ever.

Six months later my man Gilbert mounted my defense and we pled not guilty, but man, the trial was a farce. Strictly for show. The jury stayed out for forty-seven minutes, and that was forty-six minutes longer than they'd needed. How they say that shit on *CSI*? The DNA don't lie? Well they must have figured that ex-cons and drug dealers like me can't help *but* lie, and four days after my trial began I got convicted and sentenced to death by an all-white jury of my so-called peers.

Tell us why? The question sat on everybody's lips. What kind of man could do something like that to a baby? They stared hard into my eyes, trying to find the beast that lurked inside me.

Deborah. Mama. Strangers. To this day everybody still stares, and everybody still wants to know.

Why?

I just laugh.

Why? Shit, you tell *me*! I got a shitload of my own whys. But hey. I ain't never been the type to buck fate or throw up a whole bunch of bullshit excuses, so sitting here in the death house with the clock ticking down on me, why start bitchin' up now?

Three years and nine months.

I've seen men die in prison from the monotony of it all.

You get mind-fucked by the sameness of this shit. Day in, day out, month after month, year after year. Death row gives you a whole lot of time to think. Time to figure shit out, or at least to try. Regrets? No matter what they're saying about me out there, I *am* human. I've got a few.

"Drop everything," I told Gil a few weeks after my trial when the second set of DNA results came back conclusive and all the evidence still pointed straight at me. Deep inside I knew what it meant, but I just didn't want to know. "Just forget all this shit and let it be."

Gripping the lab sheet, the news rocked me in my nuts and sat me down hard, and I couldn't find enough strength to leave my cell for a week. Exactly what the hell *had* happened that night? I mean, I admit to smacking around a couple of females before, Terrie included, but out of all the grimy shit I'd done in my life, I had never hurt nobody's kid. Never.

But the DNA said I did. The proof was staring right at me in black and white.

I couldn't eat for a week. Couldn't sleep, either. Couldn't stop searching that black spot, that drunk-ass night that I'd lost. I couldn't stop seeing them autopsy pictures of Arielle's banged-up little face, either. Her torn-apart little body. What kind of man could do some shit like that?

"Fuck it, man," I'd told Gil. "No appeals. Let's get this shit over with."

"You don't wanna do that," Gil warned. "Ride it out, Isaiah. You say fuck your appeals and it's the death house for sure. Stick around and ride it out. Anything can happen while you wait for the appellate courts to review your case. They might find something and give you two dimes, maybe a two and a quarter. Let's just ride this one out together baby and pray for the best."

I shook my head.

"Isaiah," Gil had said, and for the first time since I got locked up I saw defeat in my boy's eyes. "You don't have to *remember* killing nobody in order for them to bury you up in here. You fuck around and drop those appeals and they'll fry you faster than shit, man. Executions are back on the menu, my brother. They convened a special council to lift the moratorium. They're dusting off that chair just for you."

No appeals, I told him. And fuck all the ones that were automatic too. I had a legal right to drop them. Yeah, I knew what it looked like, but who said I wanted to beg a bunch of Uncle Toms or honkie-ass judges so they could sit around a table and play games in my name?

Just back the fuck off, I'd told Gil, and I meant that shit. Death row wasn't badder than me and it couldn't get in my head, neither. I didn't give a fuck what the state of New York said. I'd walked in here a man, and I was leaving out of here one too. So fuck all them bullshit appeals and tell 'em to bring this shit on! My life was *mine.* It belonged to *me.* And as long as I was giving it there wasn't a motherfucker on earth who could take it away.

TICKTOCK
7 O'CLOCK

DELLA *"It's gone be all right, Della,"* Bo comforted *her as she lay writhing in the throes of labor. He wiped the sweat from her head and held her hand as she clutched the bedsheets and cried out in pain. She was lovely and small-framed except for her huge, misshapen belly. It bulged on one side and flattened on the other, firmed, then softened, pushing its load southward as her body prepared to expel its cargo prematurely.*

Bo gave his wife a reassuring smile as he ran his calloused hands over her slender arms. Childbirth scared the hell out of him. He'd been here before, with his first wife. They'd whisked

15

her into the delivery room moments after Bo carried her into the hospital, but neither she nor his twin sons had survived the ordeal and Bo had walked out of there empty-handed, a lonely, brokenhearted man.

But time had passed and today would be different. He could already feel it. Carrying three babies was one hell of a load, but his new wife, Della, was young and strong. She'd spent the past six weeks on bed rest, reading and singing to the babies and asking God to bless the three little miracles growing in her belly. Right now excitement shone in her eyes, even through the pain, and as scared as he was Bo couldn't stop grinning either.

He wiped her face again and then turned the handkerchief on himself. He was a muscular, big-boned man with wide shoulders and big knuckles. For nineteen years he'd worked as a brick-layer, and at forty-five he was still fit and strong, although his midsection had thickened over the past three years due to Della's Southern cooking.

Bo had waited a long time to take another wife. Mostly out of grief, but also out of fear. Most women wanted babies, and Della had been no exception. He'd met her at a christening ceremony for a neighbor's child and they'd locked eyes for long, soulful moments.

"She's just a baby," he chided himself, using his hat to cover the erection that had suddenly loomed large in the church house. She had a sweet, youthful face and a slender body that was pert *in the bust and full in the hips. Bo had tried to pull his eyes away, but she wouldn't let him. Child, hell. The set of her chin and the smile on her lips said she was all woman and challenged him to treat her like anything but.*

Della Johns was a peach. A sweet Georgia peach. She came from a superstitious clan of farmers and bricklayers who should have had their heads shoved up their backwoods asses. Her father had been a nut job. Too many loose screws and not enough bolts. Snuck around raping and killing young women till he got hold of some white girl and her people caught him in the act. They cut off his dick and strung him from a tree in the middle of the night, then set him on fire and watched him burn.

Della was just a child when her father did his killings, but that didn't stop the townsfolk, and even members of her own family, from shunning her. They said she looked just like him, and they treated her real bad, making her grow up suspicious and fragile.

Weeks after meeting her, Bo had swept Della up in his arms and held her close. You might wanna think twice, her sister-in-law had warned him. Them Johns is coo-coo. There's a whole lotta bad blood running through that gal's veins. But Bo went right on. It didn't matter none to him what nobody thought about his brown-skinned girl. He moved her into his one-bedroom tenement, then married her two weeks later. Her people got riled when word traveled to Georgia, but when they heard all the stories about Big Bo they quieted down right quick. His brick-hardened hands were legendary, and he was known to snap a neck with just one twist. Nah, Della wasn't worth no fight, her people decided. Besides, who wanted to tangle with a big black New York niggah who they said carried two pistols and fought like a bull?

Bo had done all they accused him of and more, but he'd given up those nights of hard drinking and even harder fighting when Della came along. Half-girl, half-woman, she was like a tiny bird trembling in his hand, a sweet nervous creature who needed protecting. And no matter what life brought them, Bo had sworn to do just that.

On the bed Della moaned, her legs thrashing from the pain. The room seemed too crowded as the high-risk obstetrics team prepared for their tasks. A young nurse monitored readings on a beeping machine, while another slid her hand into a rubber glove and shooed him out of the way.

"Okay, Mr. Blackwood," she said sweetly. "It's time to check on Mother now. Can I ask you to stand near the foot of the bed, please?"

Bo stepped aside. Far enough to get out of the nurse's way but not so far that Della couldn't feel him or reach for his hand if she needed him. Bo was swollen with love and anticipation. Fear too. The time between her pains was shorter now, and he knew it wouldn't be long before his sons were in his arms.

Bo would have liked to get Della pregnant three or four more times. Ten babies wouldn't be too many for him. Of course he hadn't told Della this. Not while she was busy struggling with backaches, swollen feet, a widening nose, and a blackened neck. But later, Bo knew. Later on there'd be a lot more babies for him and Della, and he was excited about living the rest of his life as the father of her children.

Bo watched as the nurse slid her hands under the sheet and reached toward Della's pelvis. Despite the sweat rolling from his armpits, he felt chilled. Time was money in the construction business, but he'd managed to take off a few afternoons and go with Della to her labor classes. What he'd seen on those films was enough to bring a grown man to his knees, and Bo widened his stance and braced himself for what he might glimpse if that nurse feeling around in there messed around and snatched that sheet back. But she didn't. Instead, her eyes rolled upward as she probed Della inside, her concentration focused on what her hands felt. Bo didn't breathe a lick until the nurse withdrew her hand and removed her glove then glanced at Della with a warm smile.

"Any time now, Mother. You can start pushing at any time."

Della never could stand Shyne and she wasn't ashamed to say it neither.

That boy had brought so much grief into her life that the thought of him leaving this world gave her little more than a deep sense of relief.

She glanced out the window as the northbound train sped toward New York's Penn Station. Her shoulders were tense and her left eye twitched.

"You'd better catch a train back, Mama," Shug had told her. Della had been visiting her cousin in Baltimore, and the early morning call from her son had cut into the peace she'd been enjoying along with her cup of coffee. "I've got a ticket waiting for you at the Amtrak station. Michelle just called. The governor denied my petition, and I think we ought to be there just in case Shyne doesn't change his mind."

Della had shrugged and switched the phone to her other ear. "I already told you I ain't going up there, Shug. My eye been jumping like crazy, and that's a sign. I'm staying with Jeanne until Sunday. I'll be back home after that."

"Sunday is gonna be too late. They have him scheduled for midnight tonight."

"Well, that's when I'll be back. On Sunday."

"He's your son, Mama," Shug said quietly.

"And he's your brother. You can go. But I ain't."

"He's your *son*," Shug repeated. "And if they're gonna

kill him we both need to be there to support him with our love. To help ease him through it."

"Help Shyne?" Della sucked her teeth. "I washed my hands of that shit a long time ago. If it wasn't for you I would have walked away from that boy and never looked back."

Shug sighed, but his next words came out sounding like a politician's. Smooth and practiced.

"Don't be like that, Mama. He needs you. We both do. Besides, there's gonna be cameras and microphones everywhere. You know they hound me almost as bad as they hound Obama. How would it look if Shyne walked into that death chamber and his own mama wasn't there? Can you imagine what they'd be saying about us in the newspapers? In the blogs? They'd raise hell, Mama. I'm running for mayor, remember? Something like that could smear the final black mark on my campaign."

Della grumbled something under her breath that her son didn't catch.

He tried again. "Just think about the press. I can't go to the bathroom in this city without somebody sticking a damn microphone up my ass. And you saw the way they swarmed your place the night the police came for Shyne. They stayed camped out on your lawn for almost a month. If you don't show up for something as big as this they'll take it as a sign that our family bond is weak. There'll be all kinds of shit-talking and speculating. Court TV, CNN, hell . . . you saw how Nancy Grace tried to dog me after Shyne was arrested. It didn't matter what I said, when they go for your throat they don't give a damn about the facts. It's called media madness. Gone are the days of responsible news reporting. Today it's all about the ratings. If they can't find the facts, they simply make them up."

"They not supposed to do that," Della mumbled.

"But they do," Shug said quietly. "They do that and a lot more. Look, Mama. Shyne's conviction almost buried *my* political career, but it was damn good ammunition for a lot of other politicians. That was an election year, remember? The governor lifted the moratorium just so he could win points with his constituents. There were five other children raped and killed in New York City around the time Shyne got arrested. Three little black girls, one white girl, and the last one was Puerto Rican. You wanna know why their killers didn't get the death penalty? It's because a black man killed the black kids, and a white man killed the white kid and the little Puerto Rican girl.

"Shyne was a black ex-con convicted of killing a white woman and raping her lily-white child. No matter how much she screwed up her life, Terrie and her daughter had blond hair and blue eyes, and New Yorkers are fed up with these types of crimes. That's why they voted to bring capital punishment back. There was no way in hell Shyne could have gotten anything less than death row."

"Well you ain't Shyne. Nobody should even partner him with you."

"I've never tried to hide the fact that Shyne is my brother. But when I spoke up for him it sure sent a lot of folks I thought I could count on running toward the hills. They packed up, jumped off my ship, and backstroked to the other side as fast as they could. But I ain't mad at them. This is politics and that's the way it goes. Besides, there are a lot of people out there who just aren't ready for another black mayor in this city. So if we show them the slightest bit of division tonight it'll be just what they need to finish me off. They'll paint a picture that says Shyne must really be worthless if his own mother turned her back on him, and then the next thing you know they'll be hinting around that since me and him have the same blood, whatever evil thing is wrong with Shyne might be wrong with me too."

That was all Della needed to hear, and two hours later she had stepped out of a taxi at the Amtrak station and climbed on the first thing smoking and heading north. Shug had purchased her a first-class ticket in a private compartment, and Della sat quietly and allowed herself to be lulled by the rhythm of the train as she relived the events surrounding Shyne's crime and his arrest just four short years earlier.

Her front door had flown off the hinges on a Thursday evening.

"Police!" they had shouted. Their battering ram was swung, guns were pointed, and badges were flashed.

"Isaiah Blackwood. Where is he?"

Della had trembled as they swept through the airy condo Shug had purchased for her, tracking dirt on her floors and flinging furniture out the way as they went.

You should have followed your first mind, she chastised herself for allowing Shyne to even darken her doorstep. Everywhere that fool went he dragged trouble along behind him, and when he'd shown up at her apartment she'd had a mind not to let him in.

She wouldn't even try to guess at what Shyne had done this time. Instead, she pointed down the hall and stepped out of the way, worried mainly about Shug. This wouldn't be the first time the police had hunted Shyne down on a bust, but when Della learned what Shyne was being arrested for, she had closed her eyes and prayed to God that they'd put him so far under the damn jail that this time it would be the last.

While the cops tussled with Shyne in the back room, Della had peeked out the window and glimpsed the television vans full of local news reporters and cameramen. She cursed under her breath. Shyne was like a cancer on them all, especially Shug. The white man didn't have to plot and scheme and try to bring a good black man down. Shyne was doing that all by himself as he killed his brother's political career one criminal act at a time.

It pained Della, this burden of his blood that Shug was forced to bear. He couldn't help who his brother was. While Shyne had been out on the streets lying and stealing and running back and forth to jail, Shug had swept floors and parked cars to pay for his college degrees, first from Hofstra University and then from Brooklyn School of Law. Della just couldn't help hearing that old Sly and the Family Stone tune in her head. One child loved to learn and the other child loved to burn. That about fit Shug and Shyne to a tee, and for the millionth time Della asked God why she'd been chosen to bear such a piece of rotten fruit.

There had actually been three of them.

Gabriel, Isaiah, and Ezekiel.

Shug, Shyne, and Shadow.

The three sons of Bo Blackwood, that big, strapping black man who had snatched Della by the heart and made all her dreams come true. Shug and Shadow had been more than any mother could ask for. Sweet, handsome, good boys.

But that goddamn Shyne?

Plain evil. He'd come into the world ruining lives. Trouble had ridden on his very first breath. Della's labor was hard, and after many hours the doctors finally had mercy and injected her with a painkiller in her spine. First her sweet baby Ezekiel was born, then Gabriel had slid out right behind him with no problem at all.

But that last one . . . Isaiah . . . the minute her husband laid eyes on him all kinds of hell had broken loose. Della's ears had tingled and she felt a strange energy emerge with this baby. A rotten smell seemed to fill the room and she closed her eyes and pressed deep into the pillows, her skin crawling from head to toe. Even the doctor felt it. One minute the thin white man had been urging her to bear down, and the next minute he'd shrank back as a bucket of shit seemed to hit a fan and the loud thump of a body colliding with the floor made her eyes fly open.

Bo had gone clean down. The sight of the last baby had rocked him on his heels, and his legs had folded. One of the nurses had screamed. Another one bent over and called out Bo's name. Della had struggled to sit upright.

"Bo . . . ?" she called out hoarsely, a fear-filled question mark trembling in her voice. The joy of her moment had been lost, the babies temporarily forgotten. The room was a blur of moving bodies. The babies were rolled out in incubators, and a stretcher was wheeled in. Della screamed out loud as they lifted her husband onto the white sheets. Bo was a big, muscular man, and it took four male nurses to hoist him. Their faces had been sweaty and grim as they worked on him. She saw the urgency in their actions and felt the desperation that permeated the room. Her man was hurt real bad. His mouth was slack. An egg-shaped bruise was rising on his temple, and nothing on him moved.

"Bo!" Della stretched out her arms as another scream of anguish tore through her. She fought against the hands that sought to calm her, the babies forgotten. It was all about Bo for her. Della's man was down, and that was all she knew.

There was hushed muttering from the nurses and a collective shaking of heads. Della picked up on their despair and screamed again. Moments later there was a slight sting and then a burning on her upper arm. Her cries became fainter but no less anguished. *Bo* . . . she wept through tears as the drugs wrapped her mind in a warm, gentle wave. Something's wrong, she thought, as she spiraled toward the dark, her ears still ringing out a warning. Something evil had entered their lives. Della's man was hurt. Hurt bad . . . and it was the sight of that last baby that had done it.

Raising three boys in the heart of Brooklyn was no easy feat, especially for a young widow. Bo's death had crushed Della and left her in a state of misery and grief.

"No. Hell damn no," is what she'd said when the doctors told her Bo had fainted at the sight of her blood, then hit his head on the metal corner of a heavy equipment cart and cracked his skull.

Della shook her head and tuned them out. Her ears hadn't been ringing for nothing, so she knew damn well the sight of blood wasn't what had killed Bo. Couldn't have been. A big man like her big Bo? As strong and able-bodied as he was? That wasn't no simple little faint that had sent him down to the ground. It was that damned baby, she insisted, and try as they might nobody could convince Della otherwise.

Bo lay in a coma for nine days with Della steadfast at his bedside. The babies were being cared for upstairs in a neonatal unit, and she had to be coaxed into visiting them.

"They could benefit greatly from your breast milk," one of the nurses told her. "Preemies especially need it. Of course, you won't be able to nurse them right now, but I can help you learn how to use the pump and we can store it until they're ready for it."

Della had considered this briefly, then shook her head and declined. When it came down to taking care of her babies or soldiering for her man, Della chose Bo. She had three sons, a set of twins and a single birth, but only one husband. It was better to give the babies some infant formula and let her milk dry up. Her Bo was going to wake up one day, and she planned to be right there by his side when he did. She wasn't about to leave him alone long enough to pump several times a day, and that last baby didn't deserve her breast milk no way. She couldn't rightfully give it to the other two and deny it to him, so they all went on a special infant formula designed for their sensitive digestive systems.

Della spent a week sitting vigil over Bo's comatose body. She ignored the whooshing sound of the ventilator that breathed for him, and instead Della prayed over him, talked to him, pleaded with him, sang to him, and even lay down beside him and let her tears wash over him.

She was asleep in an armchair beside him one morning when his doctor entered the room. He touched her arm, and Della sat upright, startled as a bright sun shone in through the window.

"Mrs. Blackwood," the older man said gently. His eyes were warm and filled with sorrow. He took one of her hands in his and cleared his throat. "Mrs. Blackwood," he repeated, his voice calm but firm, "Bo is gone. We've gone over his test results and repeated them several times. He has no detectable brain activity and he's unresponsive to pain or stimuli. He's simply not here."

Della saw what was coming. She jumped up and prepared to go to battle.

"This was a horrible accident your husband suffered," the doctor continued. "But Bo isn't the one suffering anymore. You have three tiny sons who need you. They have a good chance at living a normal life, but right now they need your help. Don't you think its time we let Bo go?"

"He's alive!" she shrieked. "My man is *alive*!" Her face contorted into a wild, angry mask. "I know how these goddamn city hospitals work. What?" she demanded. "Did his insurance run out or something? Now that the money's gone you wanna just up and pull the plug on him?!"

"Bo's insurance ran out three days ago, Mrs. Blackwood."

"So you gonna kill him just because you need the bed!"

"He's already dead, Mrs. Blackwood." He nodded toward the ventilator. "He's virtually brain-dead. Without that, he stops breathing. It's the only thing keeping his body alive."

Della exploded. "*I'm* keeping him alive! With my love, dammit! Those babies you got upstairs are keeping him alive! I refuse to let you kill my husband. If anybody so much as *looks* like they putting a hand on him, I'll kill 'em!"

Bo's accident was a tragedy, and to watch such a big healthy man die just as his children were being born—at the moment when his wife needed him most—was simply a heartbreaking misfortune. And even though the doctor had a great deal of sympathy for Della, her threat was really all he needed to hear. An hour later the security police had come for Della and forcibly removed her from Bo's room. She'd gone out kicking and hollering—fighting so hard that the nursing staff had to plead with the police to use restraint in handling her, reminding them that Della was fragile and had recently given birth.

The doctors were sympathetic to the young mother too. After the ventilator was disconnected, Della was escorted back to Bo's bedside where she was given privacy and time to say good-bye to her husband.

Della touched him everywhere. Her fingertips skimmed his fluid-filled flesh, rubbing on him with desperation, memorizing the feel of his warm body so she could recall it in the dark of night when she'd need his comfort most. She kissed his eyelids and his parched, slack lips, dragged both hands along his cheeks and felt his prickly beard, pressed her forehead to his and wished she could die with him.

Bo left the world peacefully, taking all the good, rational parts of his wife along with him, never knowing the effect his death would have on the life of his sons. Della was wrapped in grief but found a small measure of comfort in her new babies, mainly Ezekiel and Gabriel, the two she felt looked most like Bo.

The babies thrived and were released from the hospital when they were almost six weeks old, but with no husband and no family she could count on, three babies were a lot for a young widow to manage. Della struggled in those early days, and sometimes she got overwhelmed by their needs and demands.

She was dead tired and grateful a few weeks later when her next-door neighbor, Peggy Singleton, stepped in to help.

"You can take that one," Della said, directing the older woman toward the smallest baby, Isaiah.

At forty-eight, Peggy was a good Christian woman with time on her hands. Her own husband had died some years back, and both of her sons were out trying to conquer the world. Peggy lived a quiet, secluded life and liked it that way, but the walls of the tenement were paper-thin and she felt horrible just sitting there idle and listening to the babies wail when she knew Della was on the other side of the Sheetrock alone and struggling.

Peggy had lived next door to Bo for many years. She'd known his first wife well. She'd been an easygoing girl with a quick smile, and they'd grown close. It had been heartbreaking when the young thing went into labor and they lost her, and Peggy had grieved right along with Bo. Getting to know Della hadn't been so easy. The child was country as hell and was always going on with her thousands of superstitions. Throwing salt over the shoulder, hags riding folks in the night, breaking mirrors and bad luck, and sweeping somebody's feet and sending them to jail. These were common superstitions in almost every black household, especially if you were from the South, but the truth was, Peggy didn't care for the girl. She thought Della was too young and immature for Bo's good, but he had been a good friend and a trusted neighbor, and now he was dead. Peggy's conscience wouldn't allow her to see his wife and babies in need without at least offering a hand.

Peggy stood watching as Della lifted the other two boys into her embrace. The babies grinned and waved their arms as their young mother smiled into their gurgling chocolate faces.

"C'mon here, Mama's angels. Y'all hungry? Are my sweet boys ready to eat?"

Peggy looked down at the little one left lying alone in the crib. Since they were preemies all of the babies were rather small, but this one was extremely tiny. The runt of the litter. He stared at her through calm, focused eyes, and Peggy's heart went out to him. She picked him up with sure hands and brought his face to hers, then frowned.

The child was sour.

The stench of old milk was under his wrinkled neck. He was wet too. Damn near soaked through his too-big sleeper. Peggy eyed Della as she nestled the other babies in her arms, holding their bottles and feeding them in tandem. Those two looked clean and shiny, she noticed. But there was a level of grime on this baby, with his cute eyes and crusted chin, that certainly wasn't on the others.

Peggy took to coming over quite a bit. First every

other day, and then, when it was clear that Della was relying on her to care for the runt baby, she listened for his cries and came over several times each day.

"Della," Peggy had asked one day as she helped give the babies their baths, "how do you tell the boys apart?"

"Easy," Della answered as she rubbed soap down the back of the largest baby. "Ezekiel and Gabriel look just like Bo. His spittin' image." She glanced at the child Peggy held, Isaiah, the smallest and quietest of the three, and said with disgust, "That one there ain't nobody but my daddy, with his crazy-ass self. Them bad genes shoulda died right along with Papa up in that burning tree."

Peggy cast a doubtful look in Della's direction. There she went again with them crazy superstitions. Peggy was getting old and her eyes weren't what they used to be, but she could still see good enough to tell that Isaiah had the same strong features as his brothers.

It didn't take long for the babies to grow into toddlers, and as one could expect from three boys, they were more than a handful. Together they were mischievous and rambunctious, and it was all Della and Peggy could do to keep them from tearing up the apartment or banging into the furniture or falling down and knocking themselves out.

Peggy enjoyed the time she spent with Della and the boys. Her own sons barely called or wrote, and the last time she'd asked they told her she could forget about grandchildren for a long, long time. So she poured her love into Della's boys, tickled by almost everything they did and loving them deeply as she watched them grow.

Especially Isaiah.

The boy needed her. It wasn't that Della outright abused him, she was just indifferent to him. Day in and day out the boy ran around in a soggy, smelly Pamper. The other two never had so much as a red bottom, yet this one seemed to keep a raw, painful-looking diaper rash. It was the same thing with his hair and clothes. Peggy had to give it to her. Della was neat and she took a lot of time caring for her boys. She was good about combing their hair, keeping their skin oiled and fingernails clean, and washing and ironing their clothes, but somehow Isaiah always looked less kempt than the other two. His clothes were often stained and wrinkled, like she'd dug into the clothes hamper and pulled out something one of the other two boys had already worn and just threw it on him.

The most painful thing for Peggy, though, was Isaiah and his food.

The boy was always hungry. From the time they were infants Peggy had watched in amazement at the way

Della fed them. She'd line them up in their high chairs and dole out three large jars of baby food. A spoonful for Gabriel, who was now called Shug because his mama thought he was sweeter than sugar, one for Ezekiel, who they nicknamed Shadow since he followed the other two around wherever they went, and then, instead of offering the next spoonful to Isaiah, who Peggy herself had given the pet name Shyne because of his big bright eyes, Della would often skip his turn and leave him outraged and crying with his mouth wide open as he watched his brothers get full off what should have rightfully gone into his stomach.

Quietly, Peggy began to compensate for Della's shortcomings with Shyne. Sometimes she snuck and fed him from her own plate. He squealed when he got a little mashed potatoes pushed into his mouth, or a soft piece of biscuit rolled on his tongue from the tip of her finger. Whenever Della prepared to feed them as a trio, Peggy would hurry and snatch Isaiah up and get him his own bowl of cereal or jar of food, and she'd make sure she stuffed him until he was full as a tick so that his pitiful cries of hunger wouldn't pierce her heart through the walls all night.

If Della noticed Peggy's attentiveness to Isaiah she never mentioned it. She seemed happy to have him off her hands, and she didn't begrudge Peggy's indulgence of the boy. And on her part, Peggy grew to feel responsible for young Shyne. She could tell his cries from those of his brothers, and hearing him wail was enough to send her scurrying next door to attend to his needs.

The boys grew bigger, and over time, due to Peggy's diligence, Shyne caught up with his brothers in height and weight. They were all handsome boys. Bright eyed and quick to smile. Shadow and Shug were comfortable with strangers and made friends easily, but Shyne, Della's least favorite, was always about a step behind his brothers, more reserved, preferring to hang back and see how things went before committing himself to anything new.

"This one is gonna be a lawyer," Della would beam at Shadow's mischievous little face and predict. The boy was cute, Peggy agreed, and had a sweet personality too. But all three of them did, and Peggy thought Della babied Shadow way too much. She doled out 80 percent of her affection on him. The other 20 percent she readily gave to Shug, and that left nothing at all for Shyne.

If Della was aware of the inequities of her affection she certainly wasn't bothered by them. "He's his daddy," she'd kiss Shadow and declare whenever Peggy or someone else made a comment about her lopsided brand of loving. "I swear the child looks like Bo, walks like him, holds his head just like him . . . this baby here ain't nothing but my husband come back in the flesh. I believe God took Bo's spirit and breathed it right into Shadow as a mercy and a blessing to me in my time of grief. So if it looks like I love Shadow more, then that's because I'm loving the part of my husband that's in him too. I ain't 'shamed to say it, neither. Shadow is my heart because he's got Bo's soul."

Despite their mother's misaligned love, the boys thrived. They had each other to play with, so Della decided against putting them in preschool. They skipped kindergarten too because Della couldn't bear to be away from Shadow for a whole day, and when their sixth birthday rolled around, Peggy was relieved when Della was legally required to enroll the boys in first-grade classes at PS 81.

But when Peggy stepped into their apartment on the morning of their first day of school, she could've sworn she'd walked in on a wake.

"Who died?" she said, startled by the look of grief in young Della's eyes.

"Today is his first day," Della said, gazing at Shadow and very close to tears. "I ain't never let my baby go nowhere by himself before. Especially all day long. How you think he's gonna make it, Mizz Peggy?"

Peggy had taken the crying young woman into her arms, but there was a smirk on her face as she patted Della's back.

"Oh, he's gonna make it. No doubt. The boy will be just fine. It's his mama who I'm not so sure about."

"Isaiah can go to any room you wanna put him in," Della had told the school registrar, "but Ezekiel and Gabriel have got to stay together, you hear?"

As it turned out all three boys were placed in the same classroom, and even though they were rowdy and liked to roughhouse, they were such good-natured and outgoing kids that it was easy for them to make new friends and form bonds outside of the one they obviously shared together.

All was going well for them, and Della and Peggy were both pleased. Having Shyne in school all day was a particular relief to Peggy because it meant the boy could eat his fill of the free breakfast and lunch the school offered without her worrying about whether or not he was getting his share of food at home.

It was during the early months of second grade that things went bad. As much neglect as Peggy thought Shyne suffered at the hands of his mother, something happened one cold winter afternoon that caused a major shift in Della's affections, and years later, try as she might,

Peggy would be unable to recall Della ever again touching the boy, not even to hold his hand crossing the street, and she was absolutely sure that the woman had never in life aimed a word of love or praise in Shyne's direction again.

Thanksgiving was nearing and the tree leaves had turned orange and yellow before surrendering to the laws of nature and falling wistfully to the ground.

The boys had an air-conditioning unit in their bedroom window that had a loose, ill-fitting seal. The winter hawk was out in full force on most days, and at night the whipping wind whistled through the spaces surrounding the air conditioner, forcing cold, dry air into the room.

Shadow had been coughing quite a bit, so Della decided it was time for the unit to come out and go into storage, then the window could be properly closed and her baby wouldn't have to breathe that bitter dry wind all night long.

Peggy came over to help one Saturday morning as Della unscrewed the bolts and disassembled the mount. It took both of their strength to ease the heavy unit from its berth and carry it from the room, and when seven-year-old Shyne ran over to offer his help, his mother shooed him away. "Don't nobody need your help!" Della snapped. Just close that window and go sit your ass down."

Later that afternoon, after doing laundry and putting a pot of neck bones on the stove to simmer, Della had gone to her room and lay down to catch a quick nap. She'd taken a temporary job cleaning hotel rooms for a few hours each day and was often tired on the weekends. She had sent the boys to their room to rest as well, but it was Saturday afternoon and they were full of energy. She could hear them laughing and roughhousing just as they normally did.

"Lay your asses down!" Della yelled, and the laughter died down to a stifled giggle. Minutes later the unmistakable squeaking of bedsprings reached her ears, and Della peeped from one eye and chastised the boys again.

"Y'all better not be jumping on those beds! If I have to get up and come in there I'm gonna whip some asses for sure!"

The only one who knew to take that threat seriously was Shyne, because Della hardly ever whipped Shug, and Shadow had never been spanked in his life.

Della had barely laid back on her paisley spread and dozed off when the boys were at it again. She heard them banging against the walls and laughing, but she was so sleepy she could only ignore them as she drifted into a deep sleep.

Later, when asked, she would be unable to pinpoint exactly what it was that had awakened her. It wasn't really a sound. It was more like a feeling. A presence. Something had touched her sleeping soul, and suddenly the scent of her husband was in the air. Della had stretched out her legs and moaned, struggling awake as she felt Bo's calloused hand slide down her bare arm and heard his gentle timbre in her ear.

"Be strong, baby," Bo whispered, his voice hoarse with sadness. Della bolted upright. Her chest heaved as she cocked her head and trained her ears on the room next door.

It was deathly quiet over there and an icy finger of dread crept down Della's spine. She swung her legs off the bed and ran from her room in her robe and bare feet, and the moment she opened the door, she knew.

She took inventory in a flash. Two boys. One by the window, the other near the tussled-in bed. Her eyes swept the entire room in less than a second. The beds were empty. As were the beanbag chairs. The closet stood open and the clothes she had carefully ironed and hung up had been pulled down to the floor. The blue-checkered curtain waved like a flag as the biting wind rushed through the open window.

Her feet wouldn't move. Her throat closed up. As bad as she wanted to rush over to that window, Della's feet just wouldn't move. Someone screamed outside and all Della could do was pray. *Please, Lord. Not him. Just don't let it be him. I'll give up everything and everybody else, but please don't take my Bo from me again.*

It was God who moved Della's feet toward the open window. Her mind had shut down and her heart barely beat. Yet God commanded her body and sent her across the room to lean out of the open window and look down on the street below.

Her baby was down there.

Flat on his back with his arms outstretched like an angel, her little Shadow lay in a puddle of blood as neighbors and passersby gathered around and peered down at him, shaking their heads in grief.

Be strong, baby.

Della heard Bo's voice in her ears once more and felt his big arms close around her as her knees gave out and she began to crumble, but just then an unimpressed voice spoke and freed something dark inside of her.

"Shadow's a big liar! He said he could fly!"

Della snapped. Her hands were like bear claws as she snatched the little boy by the back of his shirt and thrust him up into the air.

"*You* did it!" she raged. "*You* did it, goddammit, didn't you?"

She flung her small child onto the ledge, then pushed him out of the open window until his head hung toward the ground. His eyes were wide with terror as he clawed for his mother's nightdress. Della held him by his shirt and shook him brutally, the violence in her hands the only thing keeping Shyne from sailing over the edge and joining his dead brother on the concrete below.

"You killed my baby!" Della bellowed. "You killed everything I ever loved, you evil, good-for-nothing, demon-ass motherfucker!"

It was Shug who came to his brother's rescue.

"Mama, no!" he screamed. He grabbed Shyne with one small hand and beat at Della with the other.

Shyne's eyes were wide with fear. He locked his legs around his mother's waist and held tight. Straining upward, he reached out and clutched Shug too, and together they fought against Della as she tried to fling her youngest son over the ledge.

"Your ass ought to be down there!" Spit flew from her lips as Della tried to untangle the boy's arms and legs from her body and thrust him out the window. "You oughtta be down there dead instead of my boy!"

"He didn't do nothing, Mama!" Shug pleaded as he fought to drag Shyne back inside. People on the street below were looking up in alarm. A few strong men readied themselves to catch the boy, fearing Della had tossed out the first child and was preparing to toss out another.

Energized by the screaming crowd, Shug got his arm around his brother's neck and they clung to each other like interlocking links of a chain. Della elbowed Shug in the face as she tried her best to thrust Shyne into the wind, but she would've had to be as strong as a man to get them both out of that window because Shug was almost glued to his brother and he wasn't letting him go.

"I swear he didn't do nothing, Mama," Shug moaned and cried. "Please don't throw him out. It wasn't his fault, Mama. It was mine."

Della went still. She looked down at Shug, then collapsed slowly to her knees.

Crying and shaking, Shyne fell back inside the room, grateful to be on solid ground as Della turned away from him and put a gentle hand on Shug's arm. With sirens blaring in the background, she mushed her face to his and their tears mingled and fell down their cheeks.

"Don't talk like that, baby," she shushed him. "Don't you never say nothing like that again! Don't you *never* take the blame for him, Shug. And don't you never lie and say you did something bad like that again!"

Shug stood frozen against the wall. Shyne lay panting and crying on the floor. Shadow was outside growing cold on the cement, and Della was going out of her mind. She knelt beside the boys, ranting and raging with all manner of twisted words raining down on them as she stroked Shug's face and pleaded with her dead husband.

"You left me again, Bo!" she cried. Shug trembled as his mother screamed toward the open window, calling out his father's name.

"Dammit, Bo!" she wailed. "What the fuck you come back here for? Just to leave me again? Ain't I suffered enough? You gonna come back here and take my baby and then wanna tell me to be strong?"

Della was still raging at the dead as a group of men kicked in the front door and rushed inside to rescue her remaining sons.

"Bo, please don't do me like this no more, okay, baby? This shit is killing me, man. Killing me! Stay here with me this time. Don't leave me. You promised!"

Later that night, huddled together in bed with their heads under the cover, Shug and Shyne cried for their brother. The whole tragic accident had happened in the blink of an eye, and their memories were a blur as they tried to figure out how Shadow had ended up sailing out the window and dead on the ground.

"I saw him jump from the dresser then he took two hops from the bed. That's when I grabbed his arm and he sprung straight out," Shug said with guilt heavy in his voice. He had an almost-memory of yanking Shadow's shirt and swinging him toward the window, but he couldn't be sure.

Especially when Shyne insisted that Shadow had taken a different route. "Uh-uh," Shyne countered. At seven he was already fiercely loyal. He wanted to ease his brother's conscience, although it *had* been Shug who opened the window and helped Shadow fly out.

"It wasn't the bed, it was the chair. He was standing on the dresser first, then he jumped down to the chair. I think he got up on the Batman beanbag and hopped from there. Then he fell. By himself, though. Yeah, Shadow did it by himself. That's what he did."

The boys never again spoke about the manner in which Shadow had gotten onto the ledge and out of the window, but one thing they did agree on was the madness his death had brought out in their mother. Della's eyes had been scary with anger, torment, and grief. So scary that guilt and shame had flooded her sons' hearts and etched itself into their DNA. At some point during the night, Shug and Shyne had wiped away their tears and held each other tight. They stared at each other with fear and love, and agreed that for the rest of their lives they'd never do anything that would put a look like that in their mother's eyes again.

Moments after pulling into Penn Station, Della was clutching her small suitcase and standing on the street outside. As promised, Shug had sent a car for her and she waited on the curb as the driver opened her door, then placed her luggage in the trunk.

The streets of Brooklyn were wet and cold, and at home Della made herself a cup of coffee and ate a few saltine crackers as she waited for Shug to arrive. She shook her head and couldn't believe she'd let him talk her into coming home early. It had been bad enough being the mother of a murderer and having folks look at her the way they did. Della knew what kind of evil thing her son was, and had known it from the moment he was born. But walking up in that prison tonight was going to be really hard. It was *her* who had spawned the beast, and people acted like she should break down in public and cry and beg for the life of her child. Bullshit, Della thought. *Bullshit.*

Thirty minutes later she had changed her clothes and combed her hair, but only because the cameras were sure to be on her and she wanted to look good for Shug's sake. She thought about Terrie and that sweet little baby of hers and prayed Terrie's family was holding up. They were good, decent folks, and none of them deserved the heartache Shyne had put them through. Della fought back tears as she remembered Terrie and Arielle and how bitterly Terrie's family had cursed Shyne's name when their bodies were found. She couldn't blame them either. What kind of monster would slit a young woman's throat, then rape a baby and toss her over a fence to get gnawed on by a pack of fighting dogs? A familiar anger raged in Della's heart. It was a good thing Bo hadn't lived to see what kind of dirt that boy had wiped all over his good name. She had just rinsed her cup and set it aside to drain when the phone rang.

"Della, where've you been? I've been calling you for three days." Mizz Peggy was on the line and Della sighed. The old woman was now into her seventies but still spry and sharp-minded.

"I'm so nervous," Peggy went on. "Oh, my Shyne. I wish I could hold that boy in my arms! They gonna kill him tonight, ain't they? I heard them say it on the news, but I just can't believe it."

"Well you need to start believing it," Della said dryly. "Because it's definitely gonna happen."

"Well, how come you ain't up at that prison house raising hell, baby? You just gonna let them kill our boy and not make no fuss?"

"Raise hell for what? I know you ain't forgot what Shyne did to Terrie and her baby, Mizz Peggy! You do remember Terrie, right?" Della's voice was thick with sarcasm. "And that cute little baby of hers you used to like so much? They the ones you should be feeling nervous about. Shyne raped that child, you know. Sure did. Raped her so bad her insides was all busted up. Then he threw her away like trash and some dogs got to her. So no, I ain't going up there raising no hell. Shyne done enough hell-raising on this earth all by himself. Besides, I just got home a bit ago. I was visiting my cousin in Baltimore, but Shug made me come back. He says I gotta go upstate with him otherwise things will look real bad for him."

"I still don't see how they can be so sure it was him . . ." The old woman's voice trailed off and Della felt her temper rise.

"I done told you a million times, they sure. They more than sure."

"But that girl said Shyne was home with her all night, remember? I still don't see how the boy could be two places at one time. It just don't make no sense, Della, that's all."

"Who you talking about? That Deborah? She ain't no better than Shyne! She was so damn jealous of Terrie you can't believe a word she says. Deborah was just mad because Terrie and Ben was having another baby and she couldn't have her one by Shyne! You saw the way that heffah showed out on my birthday! That little slut was so drunk she couldn't remember if Shyne drove the car home or if she did. Ain't no way she could know whether he was in that house all night or not. She was passed out her damn self, and for all she knows Shyne could have left and came back twice."

Mizz Peggy sighed and spoke in a whisper and Della could tell the old lady was trying not to cry. "Poor Shyne. He never had a chance, bless his heart."

Della grunted. Poor Shyne her ass. Both boys had stayed close to their nana over the years, but it was Shug who Mizz Peggy should have been worried about. He was the one who had moved her into a nice little senior citizen complex a few years before Della got her condo, and it burned Della up that it was still Shyne who got the lion's share of Peggy's heart.

"Shyne had the same damn chances them other two boys had. He had more of a chance than my Shadow did, God rest his soul. You can quit worrying yourself about Shyne now, Mizz Peggy. The Lord is vengeful and retribution will be His. Shyne is gonna meet his maker tonight, and if there's only one dry eye in the house when they pull that goddamn switch, you can best believe it's gonna be mine."

TICKTOCK
8 O'CLOCK

JANET "It's getting real nasty out there. Are you sure you still want to drive?"

Janet looked up from the documents she'd been studying and nodded toward her assistant. Tall and cinnamon brown, Dera Dobson was elegantly dressed in a chic winter-white maxicoat and a matching white tam.

"There's a flight leaving at eight. I could have a car service zip you over to LaGuardia to catch it. You'd be in Rochester less than thirty minutes after takeoff."

Janet's smile was weak as she shook her head. She understood the concern on her friend's face. This case had touched them like none other, and after more than three years the entire city was rejoicing that the killer's day of reckoning would be coming early.

"Thanks, Dera," she declined. "I'd rather drive. I'll be careful, though. I'm wrapping things up right now and I'll be on the road before dark."

Dera looked unsure. Her gaze flitted to the crime scene photos fanned out on Janet's desk, then back into her boss's brown eyes. The brutality depicted in the photos made them three-dimensional and brought the painful images to life.

"It seems like just yesterday, huh?" Dera asked softly.

Janet stared down at her desk for long moments before answering. "Yes," she said, remembering how young and tender they'd all been back then. "Yesterday."

"I hope his ass suffers," Dera blurted, her usually reserved demeanor gone. "I want that bastard to feel every volt of electricity they shoot through him. I want his wicked ass to bleed."

Janet looked up. Like the rest of the city, she and Dera had stumbled through the firestorm of this case hand in hand, and all of them had emerged permanently scarred on the other side.

"So do I, Dera. So do I."

• • •

It had snowed almost every day for a week, and a bitter rain was falling as Janet climbed behind the wheel of her Lexus 350E and blasted the heat as high as it would go. Tugging off her red wool cap, she smoothed her brown curls and rode her brakes down the inclined garage ramp that led out to the busy streets littered with holiday shoppers who, despite the windswept rain, were filled with good cheer.

She drove slowly down the slush-caked streets of downtown Manhattan. Heavy drops of moisture rain-danced across her windshield and the rhythmic swishing of the wipers was barely noticeable as she flowed north out of the city, consumed by her thoughts.

Janet never smoked in her car—her boyfriend had allergies—but tonight she lit a cigarette and inhaled deeply. It had been a long time since she'd faced Isaiah Raynard Blackwood, and tonight she couldn't wait to stare into his eyes once again. She'd been reexamining the crime scene photos for a week. She'd read and reread the coroner's affidavit, reliving every detail both in her dreams and when awake.

Janet had spent ten years working in various capacities in Kings County's district attorney's office, and not much shocked her anymore. She'd seen the worst Brooklyn had to offer, but this case had triggered something deep inside of her and it just wouldn't let her go.

She kept one eye on the wet road and fiddled with the radio. Almost four years had passed since a pregnant Terrie Mills and her three-year-old daughter had been murdered. To the media that had seemed to be the beginning of it, this open season on pregnant women. Laci Peterson, Jessie Davis, Shamika Gray, and so many more. According to the statistics, a woman was at the greatest risk of being murdered while she was pregnant, and what was worse, the offender was almost always the father of the unborn child. Janet swallowed hard as gory images of Terrie Mills's pre-born fetus merged with some from her own past and caused hot anger to swell in her chest.

Whatever the motive, the state's case against Isaiah Blackwood had consumed Janet in its flame, and she'd been relentless in her prosecution of his crime. During the trial she'd used a multitude of sickening words to describe him. *Pedophile. Rapist. Baby killer. Woman batterer. Filth. Slime.* It had taken months for Janet to be able to close her eyes without seeing the bloody results of Blackwood's sadism. Terrie Mills had suffered greatly before dying, that was obvious. With her throat slit and fourteen deep slashes across her abdomen she'd scooted around, clutching her gutted stomach in her arms, desperate to keep her unborn child from sliding right out of her womb.

And as bad as it had been for Terrie and the fetus, Arielle, her three-year-old daughter, had suffered even worse. Janet had wept each time she examined one of the crime scene photos or read details from the twelve-page coroner's report. Blackwood had attacked the three-year-old from behind with enough force to snap her ribs. Arielle's head had been crushed and bloody, her tiny vagina violently penetrated. Her anus was lacerated and stretched out to roughly the diameter of a pickle. Her bowel had been perforated, and her organs had failed. He'd kicked her around like a football. She had a ruptured liver. A crushed windpipe. Bruised spleen. Both of her legs were fractured. Six broken ribs. Dislocated shoulder. And afterward he'd tossed her into a kennel of pit bulls who completed the job, tearing her apart and gnawing her to the bone, her lifeless blue eyes left staring toward heaven.

The brutality of Blackwood's crime was almost unfathomable, and for weeks Janet was an emotional wreck. She'd lived and breathed the case. She'd *felt* for Terrie Mills and her daughter. She'd absorbed Arielle's pain until her own bones ached and her body was sore. The hours flew by as she chased the evidence and prepared to battle the killer. Several times each day she was forced to leave her desk and retreat into the ladies' room where she cried herself dry. Alone in her apartment at night, she neither slept nor ate. Fifteen pounds fell from her curvy frame, and her boyfriend and co-workers began to worry. Janet pursued the case with a single-minded determination, pausing only when she was too exhausted to go on. Pausing mostly to cry.

The governor's office had folded under the barrage of public outrage, and the moratorium on the death penalty had been lifted. It was Janet's dedication to Terrie and Arielle that fueled her arguments in the courtroom, and her impassioned plea to try this as a death penalty case won the public's support and rallied her staff to action.

The cold rain had formed into sleet, and her tires slid as she turned too fast onto the entrance ramp at the New York State Thruway. Janet pumped her brakes and steered into a quick correction. *Don't go killing yourself now,* she chided. The last chapter of this book had yet to be written. Tonight Terrie and tiny Arielle Mills would finally have their justice. And tonight their killer would finally get what was coming to him too.

• • •

As the child of Orthodox Jews, Janet had come of age almost twenty years earlier as a mousy, slightly overweight freshman at Hofstra University. The excitement of leaving the Crown Heights home of her parents and venturing out into the world was almost more than she could stand, and after moving into the freshman dormitory she walked around campus exhilarated by her freedom.

She'd been assigned a room with three other pre-law students: Kimberly Smalls, a gorgeous African-American girl from Central Islip, and Beth Cannota and Lisa Inga, two Italian girls from Bensonhurst. They got along well, each of them burning with passion for the law, each with her own dreams of future courtroom litigations, policy disputes, and the balancing of Lady Justice's scales.

Maybe it was because they were both minorities, or perhaps it was because they genuinely took a liking to one another, but Janet and Kim found themselves paired up quite often. Even though they enjoyed a great relationship with Beth and Lisa, they took a particular liking to each other and became good friends.

Of course, there were plenty of African-Americans living in the Crown Heights area of Brooklyn where Janet had grown up, but the small community of Lubavitcher Jews seldom associated with them. There'd been quite a bit of bad blood between the two ethnic groups over the years. Each side accused the other of racial bigotry and violence, and stereotyping, mistrust, and hatred were magnified whenever they clashed over shared resources.

Janet recalled an incident many years earlier when a young black child named Gavin Cato had been playing with his cousin outside of his apartment on Eastern Parkway. A motorcade for a prominent Hasidic Jew had been driving past, and one of the drivers, a young man named Yosef Lifsh, had sped through an intersection to catch a red light. His car spun out of control and jumped the curb, striking the two children and pinning them against the building.

Poor Gavin had died instantly, and the black community had called for the driver to be prosecuted for his murder. When it became apparent that there would be no redress for the child's death, blacks in the community had rioted and taken their outrage into the streets. Sadly, a young Hasidic man, Yankel Rosenbaum, was dragged out of his car and stabbed during the riot, and his killing fueled rage and indignation from the Jews, who insisted Gavin's death was simply an unfortunate accident.

No matter how you looked at it, two people lost their lives that day, and a little girl suffered life-threatening injuries. Janet had been taught that blacks were violent, unruly, lazy, and unclean, but she'd never experienced anything to support that. She'd had secret friendships with a few black girls in Crown Heights and had even had a crush or two on some of their brothers. She loved her family and her close community of friends, but there were other aspects of the world she wanted to explore. Other peoples, other cultures she wanted to know and understand, and when looking at the beautiful, poised Kimberly, she simply couldn't internalize many of the negative things she had been taught to believe about people like her.

These sweet feelings were compounded when Kim invited her home to Central Islip for a weekend. The house was lovely, tastefully decorated, and at least three times the size of the apartment Janet had grown up in. She'd been mesmerized and amazed by the beauty and warmth of the Smalls family; a brother Kimoro and a younger sister Kimani, and Janet was also immediately drawn to Kim's parents, who took great pains to welcome her and make her comfortable.

"You've probably never had collard greens like this before." Kim's mother beamed. "Don't worry, Kim told us you don't eat pork, so I seasoned them with smoked turkey. I hope that's okay."

Janet sampled foods she'd never even heard of before,

and she enjoyed most of them. But what she loved most was the relationship that Kim had with her family. The way they were open with each other and with her as well. The endless hugs and free, unabashed displays of affection. Janet knew Kim loved music, but that evening when she sat down to the piano and played a complicated jazz duo with her father while her mother scatted in accompaniment, Janet was awestruck by the pure talent the family shared.

Sunday came calling far too quickly, and when it was time to leave she knew her life was far richer for having experienced the love of Kim's family and she was grateful that her friend had thought enough of her to allow her a larger glimpse of her world.

Of course she would have loved to have taken Kim home with her to Brooklyn as well, but Janet knew that was impossible. Theirs was an extremely closed community, and although they'd made an uneasy peace with their black neighbors over the years, after the amazing weekend Janet had spent with the Smalls family she couldn't imagine how horrible it would be for such a vivacious, outgoing girl like Kim to be subjected to Lubavitcher mistrust and treated like an outsider.

So she satisfied herself with enjoying Kim's friendship and companionship during their free time. They shopped together, ate lunch together, laughed a lot, and shared their secrets. Yes, they were very different in many ways, but both were kind and open-minded. Their friendship grew quickly and made the time at school fun and exciting.

Kim's father was a tax professional who had been investing for her college education since the day she was born. Janet's parents were financially comfortable but by no means rich. She had worked hard to earn a partial academic scholarship and supplemented the pocket money her parents sent her by working part-time in the school's computer lab.

It was there that she'd first seen Rashawn, an ambitious third-year senior, a pre-law student who seemed to spend most of his time furiously writing papers and studying case law online. He came into the lab almost every day, and Janet was immediately drawn to him. They'd started out with quiet nods of acknowledgment, but after several weeks of running into each other in the lab, the student union, and the main cafeteria, Janet worked up the nerve to say hello, and a casual conversation ensued.

Rashawn was a polished senior, and the moment he fixed his attention on her Janet's heart had fluttered. She'd been with a couple of guys before. Nothing serious, although her parents would die if they knew she had lost her virginity in the eleventh grade and slept with two different guys in the twelfth. But Rashawn was different from those guys. In every way. For one, he was black. Very black. With cornrows, dimples, and bright white teeth, just a flash of his grin made her melt.

He was a big guy too, the kind you'd mistake for a jock or a football star. Second, he was much older than the guys Janet had fooled around with in the past. He told her that the reason he had carried so many credits and worked so hard over the last three years was because he'd had to postpone college for a year so he could work and save money for his tuition. His plan was to cram four years of course work into three, and so far he was on track to graduate the following June.

Janet was mesmerized by the young man. Rashawn was perhaps the most handsome guy she'd ever met, and the way he looked at her with those dark, piercing eyes and flashed those brilliant white teeth made her blush so hard she thought steam might shoot out her ears.

She lived for the days he came into the lab during her shifts, and found herself sad and moody when his schedule varied and he failed to show. She was having a one-sided love affair, and she shared her fantasies with her roommates, as young girls often do, confessing only that she had a crush on the most handsome man on campus without revealing his name.

Thoughts of Rashawn teased Janet in her dreams and she convinced herself that she was growing on him too. True, he had never gotten personal with her, or asked for her phone number or a date, but he did seem genuinely happy to see her whenever their paths crossed, and once, when she received a care package of home-cooked foods from her elderly grandmother, Rashawn had seen her struggling out of the mail room and volunteered to carry the heavy box upstairs to her room.

Janet had practically floated beside him as they entered the freshman dorm. She couldn't wait for her roommates to get a glimpse of him, although she'd never reveal that he was the object of her fantasies.

Lisa and Kimberly were in the common room when they walked in.

"Where should I put this?" Rashawn had asked, carrying the weighty box like it contained no more than a pair of gym shoes.

"Right here." Janet had blushed, leading him over to the shelf where she kept her hot plate, silverware, and canned food items. "Thank you so much," she told him as he set the box down and prepared to leave. She glanced at her roommates with a devilish look in her eyes and was greeted by a look of awe and astonishment in theirs.

"Where are my manners?" she said with a nervous laugh, then turned to her friends and said, "Beth, Kim, this is Rashawn. Rashawn, these are two of my room-mates, Beth Cannota and Kimberly Smalls."

Janet could clearly read the thoughts running through her roommates' minds. They were as taken by Rashawn's awesome physique and dark good looks as she was, and they grinned at her in excitement and approval. But when she turned to Rashawn, Janet was shaken by the look of rapture on his face. She followed his gaze, which rested squarely on Kimberly, and suddenly Janet felt pale and mousy in comparison.

"How you doing?" He gave Beth a distracted nod, then focused on Kim again with a broad, gorgeous grin. "What's up, sweetheart? You know how to cornrow?"

Janet's heart turned into a block of ice. And as Kim giggled and nodded and Rashawn jotted down his phone number, Janet stared into the face of her beautiful black Adonis and felt utterly forsaken.

Kim braided Rashawn's hair at least every other day. They did other things together too. Janet was deeply hurt. And angry. She walked around in a funk for two whole months, and when she went back to Brooklyn over the Christmas break she looked more like a grieving widow than a vivacious college freshman.

Her family grew concerned.

"It's first-year stress," her father said, patting her mother's hand. "She's on a partial scholarship, remember? That means she has to work much harder than everyone else."

"I think she really misses me," her mother surmised, shaking her head. "We've never been apart for this long before."

Janet sulked around the house and allowed them to think what they wished, but truth be told she was suffering from a bad case of jealousy and rejection. Not only had something sparked between Kim and Rashawn on that fateful day, but the spark had grown into a raging flame, and within weeks the two of them had become a hot item.

A dozen knives had twisted around in Janet's stomach as Kim shared the details of her and Rashawn's private time with her roommates. Janet was forced to learn vicariously the taste of Rashawn's tongue, the grip of his hands, the girth of his dick, the depth of his thrust.

All night she'd listen to Kim and pretend to laugh and squeal along with Lisa and Beth, who by now had their own boyfriends as well. But beneath her blankets she'd twist her toes and dig her fingernails into her thighs to obliterate the pangs of envy that radiated from her heart.

You're on a campus full of cute guys, she'd tell herself in calmer, more rational moments. *Just find somebody else.* But for her, there was no one else. Sure, other guys were interested in her and some even pursued her for dates. Blacks, whites, and a few Asians too. There was a racial revolution going on in America and everybody wanted to date someone who looked as different from them as possible. Everybody except Rashawn. He was "sprung" as Kimberly would say. Completely enraptured by her dark skin, dazzling smile, and long braids. The two of them had such similar coloring and features that they probably shared some common ancestors from a long-lost tribe.

Rashawn still spent a lot of time in the computer lab, and try as she might Janet was unable to purge him from her heart. She tripped over words when he greeted her and went out of her way to reboot his machine or to change the paper tray in his printer or guide him through a difficult graphics program. She was painfully aware that she loved him, and his preference for Kimberly only pained her even more.

It was two nights before spring break that it happened. It was close to eleven and the lab was empty except for the two of them. Rashawn was working furiously to complete a paper as part of a project that was due the next morning.

"Can you give me about fifteen more minutes?" he'd asked, glancing up from his screen with an apologetic grin.

Janet would have given him a kidney if he needed it. He didn't even have to ask. She'd nodded and smiled, then gone back to reading a case study. Fifteen minutes later she'd looked up to find Rashawn still hunched over the keyboard, banging away. Her heart had melted. There was something about his serious-mindedness that excited her. He was purposeful and focused. Goal oriented. The kind of guy that would make a great husband, she knew. Someone who could be counted on to pursue his dreams and build a wonderful life for himself and his family.

Without thinking, Janet came out of the reception cubicle and flipped the light switch. She took two long steps until she was standing directly behind Rashawn, and when he glanced up at her with a small, questioning grin, she lost control.

Placing her hands on his broad, ironlike shoulders, Janet inhaled, then lowered her head in the near darkness and kissed him. First on the nape of his neck, then on his earlobe, and as he turned toward her, deeply on his lips.

His lips were juicy, his tongue strong. He did things to her lips that no other man had done, and Janet dove into his mouth with abandon, eager to prove him wrong in his choice of girlfriends.

She was like a dry sponge. Ready to soak up anything he gave her, as pliant and as submissive as a slave. Without words or any apparent affection, Rashawn lifted her skirt and pulled her panties aside. He thrust two fingers into her sharply, chuckling as she gasped out loud.

"Let's get on the floor," Janet urged. She wanted him on top of her, digging and pounding. Giving her exactly what he had given Kimberly. Making her feel everything Kimberly had felt.

He chuckled. "The floor? You would wanna get down like that, huh?"

Janet was compliant as he pulled down his sweatpants and freed his dick. Even in the darkness she could see that it wasn't some huge, monstrous organ that every black man supposedly possessed, but it was still the most beautiful thing she had ever seen.

Her pale ass shone like a moon as he turned her around and grabbed her by the hips. He pulled her down to his lap in a quick, violent motion, and before she knew it she was impaled upon him, her flesh shivering as she climaxed just from being entered.

Janet worked overtime that night. Rashawn lifted and slammed her into his lap over and over, his fingers leaving her hips only to pinch her nipples or slap her ass, the cracking noise exciting her in her desperate need to love him.

There, she told herself as he flung her to the floor face-down and bucked into her so hard her pelvis was bruised as it painfully slapped the ground. *I bet he doesn't love Kimberly like this.* She was like putty as he turned her over and inserted himself in her mouth. He made her suck for a while, then he withdrew and pushed her legs over her head and plunged into her ass.

It was brutal and erotic. Degrading and orgasmic. Rashawn wore a look of disdain on his face as he fucked her in ways Janet had only heard about, and she climaxed seven times before he finally bit down hard on her tender breast and exploded inside of her.

Janet lay panting beneath his sweat-soaked body, a smile of triumph on her flushed face. She'd gotten him. She'd gotten him. He'd fucked her like a wild man, and it was the absolute best thing she had ever experienced in her life.

To hell with Kimberly, Janet thought as she savored the strange, exotic combination of his scent: hot sex, a black man, and the hair grease that her roommate had so lovingly rubbed into his braids. Her hands were full of desperate love as they flitted over his wide back, the hard muscle of his ass, and his stallion-like thighs.

Janet didn't know what tomorrow would bring, or how they'd explain things to Kim or how they'd explain it to themselves, even. All she knew as she lay there beneath Rashawn with his black dick still rigid and jammed deeply between her walls, was that she definitely wanted some more.

If Janet thought she'd had it bad before, she was much worse off now. Rashawn's visits to the computer lab, once as regular as clockwork, became sporadic and unpredictable. She never knew when he'd slip in to do his research, and often Janet would arrive to work her shift just as he was gathering up his papers and books to rush out the door and leave. She played Twister with her co-workers, trading work dates and times, doing everything possible to land on Rashawn's square. She figured out his course schedule and cut her own classes so she could be standing outside his classroom when his ended. She'd do anything for a glimpse of him, for a few words, for just a hint of acknowledgment in his eyes.

Occasionally he found her. On those late nights when

Kimberly was busy studying or doing community service work to qualify for her future sorority, Rashawn would slip into the computer lab right before closing. When the coast was clear, and every other student had gone for the night, he'd appease her, fucking her brutally in painful, degrading ways, handling her body with stark detachment as though she was simply a quivering mound of flesh to batter as he pleased. And always, no matter how perverse his demands or which way he wanted to have her, Janet complied. In fact, the colder and more distant he was, the harder and more frequently she climaxed, her pale fingers raking and kneading his dark flesh as she strove to get enough of his scent in her nose, his taste on her tongue, his cruelty in her heart.

From the first night she'd seduced him, Janet knew that this Rashawn addiction had totally skewed her judgment. She had told him that she was on the pill, but that was a lie. She knew he wrapped it up with Kimberly, but only because Kim demanded he come equipped with plastic, and insisted that he wasn't fine enough to warrant her getting pregnant or catching an STD.

Janet had thought about asking Rashawn to use a condom once or twice, but she in no way wanted to nag him about anything that might equate her with Kim. And besides, their time together was so brief and unpredictable that once she had him in the heat of the moment she was reluctant to disturb the mood by asking for anything other than the tidbits of physical contact that he was willing to allow her.

Janet knew something was wrong two days after she missed her period.

She had never been one to have menstrual cramps, but night after night she found herself balled up in bed, her uterus contracting and her breasts swollen and sore. Three months later she'd had one light, spotty period that lasted for three days. She wanted to believe things were okay and that stress was affecting her cycle, but then she threw up her breakfast and was unable to complete her shift in the computer lab. She'd called in a co-worker to replace her, then barely stumbled back to the dorms when Kimberly breezed into their room looking beautiful and healthy.

"Guess where I'm going today?" she said with a deep-dimpled grin.

Clenching her aching stomach muscles, Janet looked up from bloodshot eyes. Kim was brown and gorgeous in a pair of off-white low-rider jeans that emphasized her curvy hips and toned thighs. Her V-neck cream-colored sweater rose up above her deep navel, and her cleavage was simply amazing. Unlike Janet, who was close to flunking out, Kim was carrying a 4.0 grade point average. It just wasn't fair for the girl to be so smart and so beautiful too. Kim had it all! Why couldn't she portion off some of her good fortune for Janet?

"W-where?"

"To Brooklyn!" Kim squealed. Her double-hoop earrings dangled as she flung her hundreds of braids over one shoulder. She pulled a cream-colored Baby Phat baseball cap over her head and continued. "With Rashawn. He's taking me home to meet his moms. Isn't that a trip!"

Yeah, Janet thought, closing her eyes. A real trip. Here she was lying in bed sick and terrified over being pregnant, while Kim had just grabbed her designer purse and rushed out the door to go home with the man Janet loved. Life was a trip, all right.

The following Wednesday Janet skipped classes and caught the shuttle bus off campus where she paid a visit to the local Wal-Mart. She was too afraid that someone might catch her buying what she came for, so after filling up her handbasket with a bunch of things she didn't need and really couldn't afford, she found a pregnancy detection kit and buried it among the Q-Tips, peroxide, shower gel, and deodorant until it was out of sight.

She had no intention of taking it back to her room, so the minute it was paid for she doubled back inside the store and headed toward the ladies' room. There, she squatted over the toilet and saturated the wand, and minutes later when a telltale pink hue confirmed her fears, Janet went numb inside.

The numbness stayed with her for three days. During that time she searched high and low for Rashawn but never saw him once. She called his phone, lurked outside of his classes, and got so desperate at one point that she was tempted to confront Kim, confess the whole thing, and demand that she tell her where their man was.

But as it turned out the confrontation came directly to her. That Sunday afternoon Janet, wearing a ratty pink nightgown with holes under the arms, was standing over the hot plate boiling a kettle full of water for tea. Her stomach had lurched and heaved all throughout the morning, and she'd finally gathered the strength to stagger out of bed to fix a hot drink.

Beth and Lisa were both in Brooklyn, and that left Janet alone in the suite with Kim. Water was running in the shower, where Kim could be heard belting out a song by Aaliyah.

Janet had just taken down a lemon-flavored tea bag when there was a knock on the door. She opened it and froze, standing dumbfounded as Rashawn stared down at her.

"Hi," she said. She reached up and smoothed her uncombed hair. It was hard to look at him. His braids were fresh and neat, his goatee trimmed, his skin clean and smooth. Janet coughed and looked down. It was after twelve and she hadn't even brushed her teeth yet. "You got my messages?"

"Nah. I'm here to pick up Kim."

His voice was cold as she stepped back to let him in.

She coughed again as Kim sang in the background.

"Umm, well. I was trying to get in touch with you," she said backing into the room. "I-I-I," she stammered under his steady, unfeeling gaze, then corrected herself. "We have to talk. There's a problem . . . umm . . . well . . ." Her next words came out in a whispered rush. "I'm pregnant."

For long moments there was nothing in Janet's ears except Kim's happy singing and the pounding of her own heart. When she finally got the courage to look up at him, Rashawn's face was completely impassive, a beautiful brown wall made of stone.

"I'm pregnant," she repeated, louder this time. "I'm having a baby."

That got him.

"By who?"

Her voice was small. "You."

He laughed and shook his head like the joke was on her.

"You white girls are all the same. You chase down a black dick until you catch it, then you try to trap us with a baby–"

"That's not true!" Janet wailed. "I never tried to trap you. Not on purpose. We were just careless, that's all. Both of us . . ."

Rashawn chuckled again. "Not me, baby. I asked. You told me you were covered. So you're not going to do this to me. I don't know what you talking about." He glanced past Janet and yelled, "Yo, Kim! Come outta that bathroom, baby. It's time to roll!"

Janet's face was crestfallen as she stared at him incredulously. She reached for his arm and he jerked away, hostile.

"Don't try to play me, baby. Find some black professional athlete to run your game on. I'm sure I wasn't the only brother hitting it, and besides, you're on the pill, remember? The last time I checked the pill was still considered birth control."

"Wait!" Janet pleaded, reaching for him again as he turned toward the door. The water had been turned off in the bathroom, although she could still hear Kim moving around. "What do you want me to do?? You always acted like you liked me!"

"I did like you. For a piece of ass. Not as the mother of none of my kids. Now get on with that. Go find your real baby's daddy. Tell Kim I'll meet her downstairs."

Janet grabbed the back of his shirt and held on.

"B-b-but there hasn't been anyone else!" she insisted. "Please, Rashawn. Don't talk to me like that. I'm having your baby! Don't you want to be with me?"

Something inside him seemed to snap, and when he turned around to face her the look in his eyes was so beastly that Janet could find no trace of the handsome young student she'd believed herself so deeply in love with.

"Why in the *fuck*," he breathed over her, "would I want to be with a chick like *you*? When I already got a real woman"—he nodded toward the bathroom where Kim could still be heard singing—"like *her*?"

Janet exploded. Snatching the full teapot, she flung the boiling water at his retreating back, wincing as it soaked his shirt and sent up a cloud of steam.

Rashawn's knees buckled as he arched his back and screamed out loud, scalded. Grabbing the bottom edge of his steaming shirt, he quickly pulled it up and over his head, and to Janet's horror she saw wide sections of naked pink flesh as patches of his beautiful dark skin peeled off right along with his shirt.

"Bitch!" he shrieked and swung on her. Naked from the waist up he charged her like a crazy black bull, and Janet fell to the floor under the barrage of his blows. Rashawn's face was twisted with fury as he stared down at her. He pulled his big fist back and smacked his knuckles dead into her mouth. Her top lip burst like a grape and hot blood spurted onto both of them. Janet couldn't even attempt to protect herself. He kicked, punched, slapped, and flung her across the room, all the while screaming in enraged pain.

Janet cried out weakly at first, then gave up and shielded her head as best she could with her hands and arms. His boot found her ribs, her chest, her back, and her stomach. Blood ran from her lip and nose, and her whole body convulsed under the force of his assault.

And then suddenly it was over. Kim was between them screaming at him to stop, shower damp and dressed only in her panties and bra. She used her body as a barrier and a shield as Rashawn raged and Janet wept pitifully from the floor.

They were both students of the law, yet neither of them went to the authorities. Janet was afraid to report the beating for fear she would be arrested herself. After all, she'd assaulted him first by throwing a pot of boiling water on him. His burns were painful and severe, and Janet was afraid that his violent assault might be seen as an understandable reaction to his intense trauma.

Yet both of them had been deeply scarred, Rashawn on the outside where it could be clearly seen, and Janet on the inside where she could never forget it. Somehow she had managed to drag herself from the floor to her bed, and there she had stayed, facing the wall and writhing in pain. She could hear the two of them out there. Kim, finally wise to what had been going on right under her nose, had argued bitterly with Rashawn as he pleaded with her to call an ambulance.

Hours later, after sitting in the emergency room and watching Rashawn suffer through his treatment, Kim was back at the dorm and ready to do battle with Janet, only to find a badly injured, defeated enemy.

"You slimy bitch," Kim had said to Janet's back. "You were the last one I thought I had to watch out for. Typical fuckin' white whores. What's so wrong with your own men that you're constantly fiending for ours?"

Janet remained facing the wall, breathing deeply through her mouth as her tears soaked her pillow. She hadn't moved in hours. She couldn't. The pain lancing across her stomach was excruciating, snatching her breath away.

"What is it?" Kim went on, so consumed by her ex-friend's betrayal that she failed to detect her pain. "White boys don't have what it takes to satisfy hoes like you in the sheets, or are you dumb-ass chicks just gluttons for abuse? You were happy to be the secret little snow bunny hiding in the back of Rashawn's closet, just as long as he gave up that big black dick every now and then, weren't you? You probably put up with shit from Rashawn that would make me kill him if he tried it with me."

Then Kim's voice softened somewhat.

"You can expect a man to act like a dog. Most of them do. But didn't you ever want more than just the little bit he was giving you, Janet? Didn't you think you deserved more? I got the movies, I got the candy, the flowers, the hand-holding, and the dates. Rashawn spent all of his free time chasing *me*. He took me home to meet his family, remember? So did you think just because the brother was fucking you in the dark that meant you were special? How could you settle for so little from him? From any man? Didn't your parents teach you any better? White girls like you are pathetic, Janet. You deserve every bit of shit some gaming brother dumps over your head."

Janet cried. She was in agony from both sources of her

pain, physical as well as emotional. Later that night, after Beth and Lisa came back, she lay in bed and listened as Kim filled them in on the sordid details surrounding Janet's betrayal. She gave them her back, pretending to be a statue, refusing to move a muscle, even when Beth and Lisa demanded she tell them if she'd ever fucked either of their boyfriends as well.

Hours later, in the still of night, Janet rose from her soaked sheets and stumbled into the bathroom as quietly as possible. Her chest, arms, and stomach screamed in pain as she squeezed her thighs together. She squatted on the toilet and panted as the urge to bear down rolled through her pelvis. Holding tightly to the sink and the toilet tissue holder, Janet tried to have a bowel movement, and it wasn't until she saw that the toilet water had turned bright red that she understood what was happening.

She screamed out loud as she bore down and the fetus slipped from her womb and splashed into the toilet. Instinctively, Janet plunged her hand into the bowl and retrieved the small, partially formed human mass. She was horrified as she stared at the tiny body, so small, so still. Janet peered through her tears and saw that it was a girl. Her heart leaped as she leaned back against the toilet tank and cradled her pre-born daughter to her breast.

Her grief was bigger than her intellect. She cried loud

and free, deep death wails that not only awakened her roommates but soon roused other students as well as the dorm resident and sent them all running to the room to see what could be hurting her so.

It was years before Janet found the strength to put the horror of that night behind her. She'd left school immediately and gone home to face her parents in shame. They'd cried with her and demanded that she tell them the name of the man who had raped and impregnated her, and then beaten his bastard baby out of her womb. Janet had refused to talk, to confirm or deny their version of her ordeal, telling them she preferred instead to put the ugly experience as far behind her as possible.

That's exactly what she did too. For a long time. The next semester she applied to and was accepted at Syracuse University, and she buried the pain of her Long Island memories deeply in the far chambers of her heart.

And for the longest time they stayed there, dormant and impotent, until almost twenty years later, on the night of July 8, when she got the call that there had been an arrest in the brutal murder of the pregnant mother Terrie Mills, and the rape and vicious killing of her three-year-old daughter, Arielle.

Janet had stumbled and cried out loud when she was handed the mug shot of the suspected killer. Her hands had shaken and she'd been forced to sit down and take deep breaths as she stared down at the smooth, perfect skin, the gorgeous lips, and into the unforgettably evil eyes of Rashawn Blackwood.

But of course it wasn't Rashawn. The man in the picture was someone different. He was heavier and something in his eyes was darker and much more sinister. He looked grimy. Like a common thug. There was absolutely no polish on him. He was far rougher around the edges than Rashawn would have ever allowed himself to become, and besides, Rashawn had shed his cornrows and ethnic edge and was now known as Gabriel. Gabriel Rashawn Blackwood, Esquire. Law degree, CEO, former Congressional Black Caucus member, and as Janet now knew, future mayoral candidate for the city of New York.

The man in the picture was Isaiah Raynard Blackwood. Aka Shyne. He was Rashawn's younger brother, and in Janet's heart and mind that connection was more than enough.

Staring at Isaiah Blackwood's mug shot, Janet shuddered. Baby killer. Destroyer of wombs. She'd never forgotten the way her daughter had slipped out of her or the agonizing pain of those killer blows to her body.

She had skewered Blackwood's ass in the courtroom, and when the short trial was over a sense of tranquility had washed over her that was similar to the aftermath of an explosive orgasm. Sticking it to Isaiah Blackwood was satisfying on all levels, but watching his brother squirm under the microscope of the press had been priceless.

Janet's impassioned arguments, irrefutable evidence, and the dogged, volatile force of her attack had elicited the highest praise at the conclusion of the trial, even from members of the defense team.

And when the verdict came back exactly the way she had expected it to, she was almost giddy with exhilaration. It was only in the darkness of her bedroom that she could admit to herself that while her prosecution had focused on vindication for the crime victims, her primary motivation had certainly been revenge. And why not? For herself and for every woman in the world who had experienced physical violence at the hands of a man. After all, Janet had been much luckier than Terrie Mills had been. Terrie had run across the wrong Blackwood brother. The pain Janet had endured was mild compared to the gutting Terrie had suffered, but both of them had lost daughters because of the viciousness of these men.

In more than twenty years Janet had never become pregnant again, even though she'd been in two relationships where she'd tried. Something more than her heart had been permanently damaged by Rashawn's fists and feet, and deep inside she still grieved terribly for the daughter she would never know.

Gabriel, Isaiah . . . there was no real difference between the two.

Don't worry, Terrie, Janet vowed as she viewed the young woman's butchered body in the autopsy photos. *I didn't get him for my little girl, but I'll definitely get him for you and yours.*

TICKTOCK
9 O'CLOCK

SHUG Gabriel Blackwood hurried through the airport with a five-member entourage flanked at his side. As a kid he'd watched a news report where Jesse Jackson was being whisked through an airport surrounded by security guards and cameramen, and sitting in the tiny living room of his tenement apartment, Gabriel's mouth had watered.

"Who's that?" he'd asked his mother, his voice high with excitement. "And what kind of job does he do?"

"Him?" Della had glanced at the television and said dryly, "That's Jesse Jackson and he gets paid to tell lies."

Young Gabriel was transfixed as he stared at the screen and watched Jesse run the show. The man was bad. He looked like a debonair black superhero and the suit he was wearing had been tailored just for him. Gabriel figured Jesse had enough bank to fly all the way to France to buy the expensive leather shoes on his feet, but even at his age Gabriel possessed an eye of discernment that most ghetto kids simply did not have. It wasn't the word "money" that Jesse Jackson's image screamed out from the television screen. It was the word "power" that came to Gabriel's agile young mind, something infinitely better, and he decided right then and there that when he grew up he was going to have the same kind of power Jesse had, and maybe even more. Watching Jesse smile, wave, deflect the press, and charm himself out of their unrelenting grasp, young Gabriel promised himself a similar life of power, and at the age of ten he was already prepared to do whatever it took to get it.

Cameras flashed as the mayoral candidate for the city of New York held his mother by the elbow and guided her down the jetway where a US Airways flight to Quincy, New York, waited. He had an early morning award ceremony the next day and his staff had wanted to charter a small plane to make the round-trip, but Gabriel had shot the idea down. His numbers were already slipping in the polls and the press was going to have a field day tonight regardless of how he traveled. But justifying an expense like that while accepting public donations for his campaign would just give his opponents more shit to talk than was already stinking up the airwaves.

Gabriel sighed and adjusted his tie. Shyne's number couldn't have come up at a worse time, and his campaign manager had advised him to put a whole lot of distance between himself and his convicted relative. Gabriel had fired the asshole on the spot. Shyne was his brother, no matter what they said he had done, and Gabriel had made it crystal clear to the public and to the rest of his staff that while his position on women and violence obviously differed from Isaiah's, they were family and not even a bid for public office was bigger than the love he had for his brother. He'd meant exactly that too, so whenever some devious reporter brought up any slick questions about his ties to Shyne, publicly or privately, the answer was always the same. Gabriel loved his brother and Shyne had his full support, come what may.

By the time they boarded the plane Gabriel had worked up a sweat. The press had been running in a herd alongside them from the time they climbed out of the limo until they were hustled through to their gate. One young reporter from a local network, a sister, had accidentally stepped on Della's heel, making her walk out of her shoe, and by the way his mother went off on the poor girl Gabriel knew there were going to be a whole lot of words bleeped out on her broadcast tonight.

A flight attendant greeted them with a welcoming smile, and Gabriel's campaign manager, secretary, and two other employees stood in the aisle as he placed Della's small bag in an overhead compartment. The plane had recently been cleaned and the circulating air smelled of fresh lemon disinfectant. Gabriel slid into his first-class window seat and waited until his mother had seated herself before fastening his seat belt. He helped Della engage her own lap belt, then took her hand and smiled.

"It's been a real long day, Mama, and no matter what happens it's gonna be a long night too. See if you can relax a little bit. Maybe get some sleep."

Della smirked and stuck out the foot that the reporter had stepped on. "The way the back of my ankle is throbbing? Who you think can sleep after getting trampled on by a damned fool?" She stared down at her foot, rotating it outward and examining her heel.

"Damn niggers just don't know how to act. That girl saw me. And she stepped on me anyway."

"It was just an accident, Mama. I'm sorry it happened but thanks for being here with me." Gabriel knew it wasn't the misstep that had his mother going; it was the fact that the offender was young, black, and accomplished. Everything Della was not. "Your being here means a lot to me, Mama," Gabriel continued. "I know it means a lot to Shyne too."

Della didn't give a damn about how Shyne felt and Gabriel knew it. Son or no son, she had turned her back on Shyne two seconds after his arrest, and the minute the press stuck a microphone in her face she let it be known that she was a mother who had raised herself a perfect son like Gabriel, and she bore no responsibility for whatever the hell had gotten into Shyne.

The press had sucked up every word Della said, and the court of public opinion came down hard on Shyne. Hell, if his own mother thought he was guilty then he probably was. Besides, one of the victims had Shyne's DNA on her body and the other one had it underneath her fingernails. The press photographers had snapped away like a bunch of shutter vultures as Della sat beside the victims' family throughout the four-day trial.

Gabriel could only watch in silence as the prosecutor glared at him, obviously getting her rocks off by butchering Shyne, while his mother made a damn fool of herself for the cameras. She'd cried and clutched hands with Terrie's mother like they were old friends, the whole time staring at Shyne like he was some strange bastard that a spaceship full of aliens had dropped off at her house.

After Shyne was convicted, Gabriel had tried to get her to make a few upstate visits with him, but Della said hell no. When she said her son was dead to her she meant dead-dead, and Shyne couldn't get a damn thing out of her. No visits, no letters, no love, no nothing.

"I'm not going up to nobody's jailhouse, Shug. Just as sure as my Shadow is dead and buried, Shyne is too."

"Why can't you at least send him a note, Mama?" Gabriel had complained. "How could that hurt? In a family you're supposed to love each other, no matter what."

"And who does Shyne love? Nobody but himself."

"He loves me," Gabriel said quietly.

Della rolled her eyes. "You love Shyne a thousand times more than he loves you," she said, but Gabriel knew this wasn't true. He knew his brother. All the way down to his DNA, and that just wasn't true at all.

But as cold as Della was toward Shyne, she relished the fact that her other son was a respected public official. Her chest got swollen with pride whenever one of her old friends from the projects called to say they'd heard Gabriel talking on the radio or had seen him campaigning on television, and Della walked around bragging on him like he was running for president instead of mayor.

It was only when Gabriel pointed out how her negative attitude toward Shyne could be used to derail his career that Della began to at least try to act like a mother and quit talking so much shit about her convicted son in public.

Gabriel knew his mother really didn't want to, but she absolutely had to be there for Shyne tonight, and Gabriel had been ready to jump in his car and snatch her straight out of her cousin Jeanne's house if he had to. He was relieved when Della agreed to accept his Amtrak ticket and take the train into Manhattan, and he hoped when the reporters jumped all over her for a statement that she would let go of all that unnecessary anger long enough to say something decent about Shyne for once.

Della startled him when she spoke, catching him in the middle of his thoughts.

"How long is this flight?"

"Two hours." Gabriel shrugged. "Maybe a little longer."

Della made a sour face. "You know I hate flying."

"I know. But with all that rain coming down, driving upstate would have been a nightmare. Flying is much faster. We gotta get in there to see Shyne before ten thirty."

"Who said I wanna see him?"

"I said, Mama. And I already told you why. You're his mother! Why can't you act like it sometimes?"

"Why you always defending that bastard?" Della blurted out. "All he ever did was bring you down, Shug. Bring you down! How crazy is that?"

Gabriel had long ago seen signs of a storm kicking up in Della and he was ready for her. She'd been steaming hot when his driver picked her up that evening, and she had heat coming out of all her pores right now.

"Mama, come on now," he said gently. Gabriel put his arm around her shoulders and laid some of that politician's charm on her that he had perfected over the years. "Don't be like that. I know how hard this has been on you."

"You damn right, it's been hard!" she said loud enough for the couple two rows up and across the aisle to turn around in their seats and stare. "I can't even turn on the television without seeing our names all over the damn news. I walk out the house and people are looking at me all funny because of him." She shook her head and gave a church woman's wave of the hand. "I'm tired of it, Shug. I can't stand this shit no more. Don't you go up in there begging Shyne to live tonight, you hear? Just let 'em do whatever they gone do so we can put this mess behind us and everybody can get some peace. Shyne too. This is what he wants, right? He told that lawyer don't fight for him no more and I don't blame him. That fool has gotta be tired because I know I am."

"We're all tired," Gabriel said, pulling Della close to him. "But we gotta hold on and keep the faith, Mama. Shyne's the one who dropped his appeals, so he can put a stop to this anytime he wants. And that's exactly what I'm hoping he'll do. All his faith might be gone, Mama. But mine isn't. I'm staying hopeful."

Della looked stricken. "You staying hopeful for what? Shyne brought this mess down on his own head! Him and that damned Deborah. He broke up with Terrie and went running straight back to that ugly girl when she wasn't nothing but trouble from the word go. Hopeful, hell. Shyne is about to get exactly what he went looking for."

"Like I said before, Mama. Maybe he didn't even do it."

"Maybe pigeons wallow around in shit and hogs fly."

"Shyne was home with Deborah that whole night."

"You still stuck on that lie? Deborah got up on that stand and lied like hell in court, but she stood right in the middle of my kitchen floor and told me Shyne left the house and got something to eat while she was sleeping, and I believe her. It's probably the only true thing that ever came out of her mouth."

Gabriel was quiet. It always came down to this. Della tearing Shyne apart and him picking up his brother's bloody remains and trying to put them back together.

"He didn't deserve a girl like Terrie," Della declared. "He wasn't even good enough to smell her pee."

Gabriel felt cold at the mention of the dead woman's name. "Terrie was okay," he said. "She was just okay."

"Damn right she was! Shyne was lucky a cute white girl like her would even look twice at his ass!"

Gabriel was pissed. So fucking what some white slut had liked Shyne? Was that supposed to validate him as a black man? He couldn't stand the sight of white women. He had absolutely no respect for them and had never met one that he didn't despise. He shook off his anger and let it ride. Della had always been a sucker for white people, and that had pissed him and Shyne both off. It might have been part of her deep-woods Southern upbringing, but Della was critical of other black women to a fault, especially if they had dark skin. But let a white woman smile at her. Della would bow down and worship her ass.

"Terrie was cool," Gabriel countered, "but she didn't need Shyne to help her be who she was, Mama. Her family is cool too, but she wasn't no angel, you know. A whole lot of foul things she got into came out in the trial, and she did a couple of bids on Rikers Island herself."

Della nodded vigorously. "Yeah, she went to jail. For messing 'round with Shyne! Terrie got arrested running behind his ass, that's what happened!"

"Yeah, okay." Gabriel smirked. There was a whole lot about Terrie that Della didn't know.

"Did you hear Shyne's lawyer when he told the jury that Terrie had already gone to jail for leaving her baby in the house alone while she went out in the streets to smoke crack? Shyne had long broken up with her and was back living with Deborah by then, but I guess everything Terrie did while she wasn't with him is somehow his fault too."

Della went quiet, but Gabriel could feel heat coming off her as fury bubbled just beneath her skin. The last thing he had wanted to do tonight was piss his mother off, and he gave himself a mental kick in the ass for getting sucked down this crazy road with her in the first place.

"I'm sorry, Mama. I know you liked Terrie and it's never right to speak bad of the dead."

"No, you're right," Della said softly, her lower lip

quivering with rage. "Shyne ain't the one who made Terrie leave Arielle in the house by herself, but he *is* the one who broke in her window and cut her damn throat, then raped her poor child and threw her to the dogs, *now ain't he?*"

Gabriel's stomach clenched and he turned toward the window. The plane had taxied down the runway and was preparing to take off. He took a deep breath and figured it was time to do some damage control. A true wearer of masks, Gabriel leaned over and planted a kiss on his mother's cheek, then after a quick glance at his watch he slid a travel pillow behind his head, closed his eyes, and thought about his brother.

For Gabriel, growing up in Della's house had been a lesson in helplessness. All the joy had gone out of his mother the day Shadow died, and Della had never stopped blaming Shyne for his brother's death. Gabriel had been the lucky one and he knew it, but Shyne was left at the mercy of a paranoid, high-strung mother who was filled with cold anger and quick to snap at the littlest thing. Della whipped Shyne's ass practically every day, and all Gabriel could do was stand by and watch, unable to help. Della could have had her sons tearing at each other's throats in jealousy if it wasn't for the bond they shared. But instead of becoming enemies they became the closest friends, and Gabriel did his best to deflect some of his mother's anger away from his brother while Shyne learned to let the rest roll off his shoulders, seemingly unaffected by the inequality of her love.

So while Shyne was often abused, Gabriel had become Della's pet. Every bit of love Della had reserved first for Bo and then for Shadow, was now poured into Gabriel. She wanted to be involved in every aspect of his life. Where he went, what he thought, and the names of all his friends. She pouted when he shook her off, and she'd stomp through the house and slam doors like he was her lover instead of her son. Shyne, who for all Della cared could have walked out the door and gotten hit by a truck, had big jokes for his brother and he rode Gabriel unmercifully about having his head stuck up Della's ass.

"Pull back, Shug," Shyne clowned him like a chump. "You got little shit balls in ya hair, man."

Della's smothering made Gabriel feel like her property and he resented it. Still, he walked around looking cool and collected, always in control, when in reality he was broiling inside. Furious as hell. Humiliated, embarrassed, and simmering. It wasn't long before Gabriel learned to dodge Della like a pro. He became slick and conniving. A good liar and an even better sneak. He did his dirt in the darkness of night, behind Della's back, and if he thought he was doing something she really, really wouldn't approve of, then he did it twice . . . but always undercover . . . his dirt was always done in the dark.

"Uh-uh," she'd tell him on summer nights as he got ready to follow Shyne downstairs to sit on the stoop. "You don't know what kinda fools is out there riding around tonight. Every time I look up there's another drive-by. Stay upstairs with Mama, baby, and I'll cut on the fan and make you some lemonade."

"Me and Shyne—"

"Let Shyne go down there if he wants to, but you stay up here."

"But why can't I go?" Gabriel would demand. He was just as old as Shyne, just as big. And just as bad.

"Because I said so," Della would say and give him a look that meant her word was final. "I gotta keep you safe, boy. You going off to college one day. Shyne is going straight to hell. You run out there messing around with them crazy boys and drinking and carrying on, and you likely to get in trouble and die with your shoes on, baby. There's trouble out there, son. Stay in here with me."

"That's all right." Shyne would laugh and whisper to his brother, "I'll handle all your troubles for you. They out there packing pussy into two-liter bottles now, ya know? I'll bring you back a whole case."

Gabriel would disappear into his room, but the minute he heard Della snoring he was out the door, right behind his brother. And Shyne, who would always be waiting for him in the darkness just beyond the stoop, would punch him and call him a baby duck, and then they'd laugh and smoke a blunt and stay up talking shit about each other's mama all night long.

Gabriel had been a real good student in high school, but Shyne was just as smart. While Della stayed on Gabriel's neck to get top grades, Shyne never paid much attention to grades because he had never been required to.

Shug and Shyne were both good-looking and well built, and neither of them ever had a problem getting what he wanted from girls. During the school day Shyne could usually be found in a dark corner on a staircase with his hands massaging some girl's ass, but Shug was popular and outgoing, seen and heard all over the school. Shyne held the hood game down hard enough for both of them, so Shug had switched gears and adopted a Kanye-like prep look that all the girls liked.

Theirs was a tough, crime-ridden neighborhood and there were plenty of opportunities to find trouble, but trouble wasn't what Gabriel strove for. He had great aspirations and left all that thug stuff for his brother, doing his best to avoid any pitfalls that might knock him off course, at least in public.

Gabriel had a plan and he was determined to work it. He was a future power player, a potential politician on the rise, and more than anything he aimed to be well noticed and highly respected. He organized a shoe drive and went around collecting almost-new shoes for children whose parents couldn't afford to buy them. He formed a cleanup committee and picked up trash from local parks. He planned a talent night at school, volunteered at a senior center, and mentored a bunch of thugs-in-the-making from the local junior high school. Gabriel wormed his way into the heart of his community and did every damn thing except kiss babies. He took extra classes in government, social policy, and debate, and when he ran for a position on the student council, he won every time.

Despite Della's attempt to smother him with her obsessive love, Gabriel learned to disconnect from his feelings as he set himself up for future success. There was a shaded side of him, though, a series of intense, uncontrollable urges that he was gifted enough to hide, even from Shyne. Young Gabriel presented the world with a convincing façade, but quite often his public persona and private behaviors were worlds apart.

Shyne, on the other hand, was becoming a true man of the streets. He hung around the projects with a group of cats who ran their world from the corners, and because he was such a big, muscular guy, he easily passed as a grown man. By the end of their junior year Shyne was so far out there that even Gabriel wasn't sure he could reach him. He was drinking and smoking blunts almost every day, and whenever he got too juiced Gabriel noticed a change come over his brother that was both ugly and dangerous.

"Man, you the last niggah who needs to drink," Gabriel told him after getting a text message that said his brother was drunk and kicking up static over in some rival projects. Still, Gabriel had put on his Tims and stormed across the street to see about Shyne. He didn't know exactly where the fight was, but as he walked through the pathways a crowd of cheering onlookers told him he was in the right place.

It was two against one, but even half drunk Shyne could handle himself in a street fight. When Gabriel jumped into the mix and started swinging killer blows too, they looked like two big black heavyweights tossing a couple of welterweight scrubs around a ring.

But fighting wasn't the worst of Shyne's trouble. He'd hooked up with a girl named Deborah and started selling drugs for one of her brothers over in Marcus Garvey. Deborah had her own crib, and Shyne moved in. They sold drugs together, got high together, and when a local fiend got crazy on Deborah one night and nearly strangled her to death, it was Shyne who came to her rescue, taking the addict out with nothing but the fury in his hands.

Gabriel remembered that night like it was just a week ago. It had been raining for days on end, and when his phone rang in the middle of the night and he heard the hollowness in his brother's voice, he'd rushed out in the rain and did what any good brother would have done. He drove down to a pier in Canarsie, and he and Shyne gave the fiend's body up to the cold waters of the Atlantic Ocean. He'd been afraid, both for himself and for his brother, but when time passed and there was never even a mention of the young man's disappearance, Gabriel learned a future lesson: when the universe opened its mouth and swallowed bums, winos, and base heads, nobody seemed to notice.

A few months later Shyne got busted and was sent to Rikers Island, and right after he got there some crazy shit went down between two blood sisters he'd been boning, and they'd both come banging on Della's door claiming they were pregnant and Shyne was the daddy.

If they were looking for some sympathy from Della,

they'd come to the wrong door. Gabriel had been embarrassed at the way his mother bad-talked Shyne. She
made the sisters come inside and sit down, then told
them they were both stupid as hell for letting Shyne's
no-good seed spill inside of them.

"Don't y'all know he got my daddy's crazy blood? You
wanna have a little one just like him running around?"
she yelled. "Is that the kind of man y'all picking to be a
father to your babies? Ain't one damn Isaiah Blackwood
already too much for the world to bear?"

Shyne got sentenced to less than a year, and he was
still locked up when Gabriel graduated from high school
and prepared to leave for college. Gabriel missed Shyne,
but he kept up with him as much as he could. Life was
strange and sometimes you got out of it exactly what you
put in. While his brother had walked on the dark side of
the street, Gabriel had spent the past four years working
on his résumé. He had applied to several colleges nearby
and finally settled on Hofstra University because they offered him the best financial aid package.

Della liked Hofstra because it wasn't too far from
home, and she made Gabriel promise to come home
every other weekend during his freshman year.

"They letting that fool brother of yours out next
month," Della told him the night before he left home. I

don't know where he's gonna stay when he gets back, but it sure won't be up in here with me."

All Gabriel could do was stare at the woman. What the fuck was wrong with her? Where else was Shyne supposed to stay when he got out of jail? Gabriel felt his mask slip and he came close to getting real with Della, but he caught himself and hid behind the amiable politician's face he'd begun to develop that would eventually come to win hearts and change minds. He walked out of the apartment and went next door to talk to Mizz Peggy.

"Nana, Shyne is coming home soon. Can he stay here with you?"

They were sitting at small round table and sharing a pack of oatmeal cookies. Hearing Shyne's name made the old woman's eyes light up.

"Always," Mizz Peggy had told him. Their nana had been in their lives for as long as Gabriel could remember, and even though he knew she loved them both, she'd always looked out just a little bit more for Shyne and Gabriel didn't blame her. If she hadn't been there to pick up Della's slack then Shyne probably would have starved as a kid, and Gabriel had laughed like crazy when his nana confessed that after all these years she never could stand his mother.

"Something just don't click with her," Mizz Peggy said

as she crumpled the empty cookie wrapper in her hands. "Della ain't right, and Shyne never had a chance with her. Never."

Mizz Peggy had also accused Della of wanting Shadow back so bad that she'd used Gabriel as a second-best replacement, and Gabriel had agreed. There had been a few times back when Shadow was still alive that Gabriel had fought for Della's attention, but Shyne never did. He had never seemed to need her, and most of the time he responded to his mother with detachment and indifference. He ignored her house rules and ran the streets at will, and by the time he was twelve he was staying out all night drinking, drugging, and partying with as many young girls as he could find.

"I'm locking my damn door and chaining it up!" Della would threaten whenever Shyne failed to make it in the house by dark. "That no-good fucker can sleep with a stray cat in an alley or go live at a boys' home for all the hell I care!"

But Shyne didn't care either. He was unstoppable. If Della wouldn't answer the door when he banged on it in the middle of the night, he simply went back downstairs and around to the same window that Shadow had fallen from and yelled for Gabriel until he woke up and let him in.

Della didn't bite her tongue when it came to chastising Shyne, and as a mother she had absolutely no shame. "Just look at Shug," she'd say, getting outright nasty and trying to make him feel like shit. "Tell me how you managed to roll around in my belly with both Shug and Shadow, and the two of them come out damn near brilliant and you couldn't find your own ass with both hands and a flashlight? If you had any smarts at all you'd grab your brother's hand and let him drag you through life because you stuck right where you're standing and Shug is going somewhere big."

Gabriel had hated it when his mother talked to his brother like that. For years she'd tried to crush Shyne with her tongue, and it was no wonder Shyne had grown up knocking the hell out of smart-mouthed honeys left and right. But no matter what chick Shyne found himself wailing on out there in the street, Gabriel had learned enough in psych class to understand that the only woman his brother was really beating was their mother.

College was everything Gabriel had expected it to be and he dove into his classes with a single-minded purpose. He'd always been Shug in the hood, and Gabriel sounded way too white, so he went by Rashawn in those days, and his goal was to follow loosely in the footsteps left by David Dinkins. He had it all planned out. He was skipping Howard–too far away–but he majored in pre-law at Hofstra and minored in mathematics. He graduated summa cum laude in three years, and afterward he was accepted into Brooklyn Law School and then started his climb toward a life in politics.

Gabriel had choreographed his every step with the utmost care. He served as a district leader before getting elected as a Brooklyn state assemblyman, then worked diligently as a city clerk for the next four years. He came from behind and stunned the opposition when he won the election as Brooklyn borough president, and at thirty-six he was right on track to become the youngest mayor of the City of New York and only the second African-American to hold the office.

"So what now?" Della had asked after he was sworn in as borough president.

"Now I find a wife," Gabriel said. "Voters want to know you're stable and committed enough to maintain a marriage before they throw the dice for you. I have to get married real quick, Mama."

Della had stared at him like he was nuts.

"Who are you going to find to up and marry you just like that, Shug? Don't you have to go out with somebody first? Bring her around to meet me and Mizz Peggy so we can see if we even like her?"

Gabriel had shrugged. He'd run through a few women over the years and while there'd been a couple of sisters who had wanted to take things to the next level, the nature of his lifestyle rendered him a loner. He'd done a little creeping too, but he'd cut back on that after almost getting caught in somebody's apartment. He'd had to haul ass out of a window half naked with about ten Borough Park cops on his ass, so he chilled with the creeping for a long time after that.

"I date sometimes."

"Not where I can see it. The last girl you brought around here was that big-rump girl from that school on Long Island. The one who said she wanted to be a big-shot lawyer but had her navel showing and all them damn braids in her hair. Who you need to look at is that pretty girl Cecilia from the bank. She's smart and cute and she talks like somebody important."

"Cecilia is white, Mama. I'm marrying a black woman."

The look on Della's face brought back old memories. She'd never gotten over her fascination with white people, and it still burned Gabriel up to listen to her put them on pedestals based upon their skin color alone. He remembered bringing Kimberly home with him and how Della had made the girl feel like she was something on the bottom of an old boot. Damn right Kim's ass had been big. Big and round, high and firm, just the way Gabriel liked them, which was one reason he couldn't understand how he could have been stupid enough to screw her roommate. He'd almost fucked his life up behind that bit of foolishness because not only did Kim drop him when she found out he'd been banging that stupid white chick who had been stalking him, he'd also gotten scarred for life when that nutcase flung a pot of boiling water on his back and sent him running to the emergency room.

Gabriel reached around and absentmindedly slid his hand over the thick sheet of scar tissue that ran from the middle of his back down to his waist. He'd been lucky that was the only hot water he'd gotten in. He had beaten the living shit out of that bitch and left her laying on the floor bleeding, and if Kim hadn't stepped in between them Gabriel knew he would have killed her. He'd been nervous as shit waiting to see if the dumb girl was going to tell on him, but when three days went by and nobody came looking for him, he knew he was safe.

Safe, but not unscarred. He'd lost Kimberly behind that nonsense, even though he'd sworn the girl hadn't meant anything to him and begged her to stay. But Kim was a smart girl. Brilliant and beautiful, and what she told him was proof that a woman like her was a keeper. There were many, many days when Gabriel kicked himself in the ass for messing around on her and getting kicked to the curb.

"Stay with you, Rashawn?" Kim had asked. Her little mini-shirt hugged the bottom of her breasts and her toned brown stomach was accented by the V of her waist. "And forget what you did to me? Forget what you did to Janet?" She'd given him a look that hurt him still, even in remembrance. "You practically beat that baby out of her, you know. The girl delivered your child alone on the toilet bowl in the middle of the night, and you want me to forget that?" She'd frowned and shook her head, and at that moment Gabriel had loved her even more. "Sorry. I just can't do that. I loved you. I had some good times with you, I really did. But you're like two different people at times, Rashawn, and right now I don't know who the hell I'm talking to."

"It's me," he had pleaded. "You're talking to the real me, Kim. I swear. The only time I can be totally real is when I'm with you."

Kimberly had frowned again and backed away. "I'm not sure you even know who you really are. I saw the way you swung on that girl. You were like an animal, completely out of control. No man gets a free pass from me after beating the hell out of a woman, Rashawn. Not even you. Honestly, I think Janet and I are both lucky we found out the truth about you when we did."

Gabriel had been devastated by Kimberly's rejection. So much so that he'd had to stop himself from chasing down that bitch Janet and stomping her ass in again. He'd kept up with Kim from the shadows over the years and was proud of what she had accomplished with her life. She'd married an attorney from Harlem and they'd established a practice together, and the last Gabriel heard it was very successful and highly regarded among New York City firms.

So while Kimberly could have tamed him and made him the perfect wife, Gabriel had been forced to accept her decision and live with his demons. Other girls had passed through his life over the years. Some of them had been really hot, and one or two he had even liked. But none had moved him the way Kimberly did, and whether it was a case of romanticizing his memories of her or wanting what he couldn't have, the fact remained that she simply wasn't meant to be the one.

But Michelle was. They'd met a few years earlier at an alumni function at Brooklyn Law School, and shortly after winning the seat as Brooklyn's borough president,

Gabriel married her at a small church in Brooklyn, never missing a beat as he continued his single-minded climb toward Gracie Mansion.

Michelle was all for his idea to throw a barbeque for Della's birthday on that fateful day in July. She'd figured out pretty early on that Della didn't like her, and despite Gabriel's assurances that it was more about her skin tone and less about her character, Michelle was willing to try anything to get in Della's good graces.

She'd gotten her sisters together to cook and season up what looked like tons of steak, hamburgers, shrimp kabobs, and franks, then invited everyone they knew and lavishly decorated the backyard of the colonial home they had recently purchased.

Things had been going pretty smoothly, especially considering that Della had been pissed when Shyne showed up with his girlfriend Deborah. Della had invited Terrie and her daughter Arielle, and the minute Deborah stepped into the yard switching her round ass, Della's attitude had turned funky.

"Why can't he ever go anywhere by himself? Every time I look up he's dragging that stupid-looking girl around behind him. My *God*!"

Gabriel had looked at Deborah as she tossed back beer after beer and grinned. Yeah, she was stupid, but the girl had an ass on her that was hard to miss. He remembered running into her a few years back while Shyne was in jail and Deborah was out on the street. Gabriel figured his brother was done with the tramp so he'd let her have twenty dollars when she asked, and Deborah had let him have more than that in return. The girl had "booty call" written all over her face, and Gabriel was shocked when Shyne picked back up with her when he got out of jail. As far as Gabriel knew, Deborah had never mentioned their little hour together to Shyne, and he sure as hell wasn't going to mention it either.

If Della hadn't kept so much drama going all day then maybe things would have turned out differently that night. As it was, her jaws were constantly yakking as she praised Terrie and belittled Shyne, until Deborah had had enough and started picking at the white girl and talking shit to her the way only a sister could.

"She is *my* guest!" Della had yelled when Deborah started verbally dominating the conversation and getting the best of Terrie. "She didn't come here to be insulted by someone like you, Deb-or-ah! So if you or Shyne have something to say"—Della pursed her lips and threw her palm in the air—"both of y'all can just talk to the hand!"

That got a laugh out of some of the guests who had been steadily drinking and playing cards, but Gabriel had felt himself broiling as Della made herself and Terrie look good at the expense of her son.

"Here." Gabriel had pushed a bottle of gin toward Shyne as they sat in his den taking a break from the heat and the shitload of company he had outdoors. "Don't mess around and get drunk or nothing, but after listening to Terrie and Mama out there I figure you earned a little something to take the edge off."

They found a cable channel showing amateur boxing matches and sat drinking and armchair refereeing for almost an hour before Michelle came looking for them and chased them back outside to the yard full of guests.

Gabriel made the obligatory rounds, talking with pockets of old friends here and there. Every so often he would look up and catch Shyne strolling back inside the house. A few minutes later he'd trot down the back steps and rejoin the party, his steps a little bit looser each time, his smile a little bit wider.

It was easy to figure out that his brother was in there killing that bottle, and Gabriel was chewing on a piece of barbequed rib somebody had passed him when he looked up and saw Shyne going back inside the house again, but this time Terrie was following him.

Gabriel's eyes darted around the yard and found Deborah deep into a game of bid Whist. Michelle was sitting with Della, smiling as she tried to ingratiate herself with the miserable old woman, and nobody noticed as Gabriel set the bone on a plate and walked across the yard and slipped into the house behind Shyne and Terrie.

He could hear them arguing as he came through the back door, and he stood against a wall and listened as Terrie talked shit about Deborah, almost repeating Della's earlier insults word for word.

"That girl is ass-ugly, Shyne," Terrie said with a short laugh. "I don't care how much booty she has, I know she can't move it under the covers like me."

Gabriel heard the freezer open and the sounds of ice clinking in a glass. He peeped around the wall and watched as Terrie stepped up in Shyne's face.

"Go somewhere with that," Shyne said, pushing her away. He turned his back on her and reached into a small cabinet above the broom closet where Gabriel kept his stash. He cracked a bottle of Smirnoff and poured some in his glass.

Terrie stepped up on him again, from behind. "No, you go somefuckingwhere. You get around her stupid ass and act like you can't even speak to me? Shit, if I hadn't let you go you wouldn't even be with that bitch, remember? She should be thanking me instead of walking around rolling her damn eyes at me. She's stupid as hell, Shyne. Even your mother said you can do much better than that."

"Gone, girl. Don't let my moms get your ass kicked in tonight, okay?"

Terrie put both hands in the small of Shyne's back and pushed him against the cabinet. "Who's gonna kick it for me?" Terrie said. "You? You gonna beat me just because I said your girl was ugly? Does that bitch know you were at my house last weekend? Fucking me like you never left?"

"Stop tripping, baby," Shyne said. "You sound drunker than me."

"So what I'm drunk? You got a whole lot of fucking nerve! Everybody under the sun knows drunk is practically your middle name!"

Gabriel could hear the anger in Terrie's voice and he wasn't surprised when she pushed his brother again. Hard. Shyne was turning around as she did it, and vodka sloshed over the rim of his glass as he caught his balance.

In a flash Shyne's free hand went up over his shoulder, then swung down in an arc as he backhanded Terrie square across her face.

Her head whipped to the side and Terrie screeched. She rushed at Shyne, windmilling her arms and cursing and kicking in rage.

"Yo!" Gabriel yelled, stepping into the room. "Don't you do that shit in my house!" he said, reaching for Terrie as she flung herself around like an idiot.

But Shyne was quick, and he banged the girl around the kitchen and smacked her four or five times in the head before Gabriel could get between them.

"Why'd you push him?" Gabriel demanded as the girl lunged around him clawing Shyne wherever she could get him. "Why'd you put your fucking hands on him?"

"Fuck you!" she screamed, her face contorted and her hair wild. "Fuck you too, Shug!" Then she glared at Shyne and said, "I'm telling your mother. Both of y'all tried to fight me up in here!"

That was the last straw for Gabriel. Before he knew it he'd slung Terrie down into a chair and held her there as he turned to Shyne. "Get up outta here, man. This bitch is crazy and I don't need no whole lot of shit out of Mama tonight."

"I ain't going nowhere," Shyne said, angry and lit with liquor. "That bitch started it. Next time I'll knock her straight on her ass!"

"Man," Gabriel said, shaking his head. The skin on Shyne's neck and arms was shredded, like a cat had gotten hold of him. "Go home and sleep it off, Shyne. Clean yourself up and sleep it off."

"Yeah, sleep it off!" Terrie shit-talked from the chair where Gabriel held her. "Sleep it the fuck off!"

Gabriel was pissed as the two of them continued throwing drunken insults back and forth. Outside, the party was still going strong, with folks drinking and dancing under the lights on the concrete patio and having a good old time. Gabriel cursed. This kind of bullshit could not be going down in his kitchen. They were still fussing as Gabriel looked from Terrie to Shyne and made a quick decision. "You gotta go," he told his brother. "You need to be outta here right now."

Gabriel slid open the window and told someone to send Deborah in the house, and as she burst through the back door he was doing his best to push his shit-talking brother out through the front.

And Terrie was just as bad.

"Yeah, leave!" she screamed as Gabriel struggled with his brother. "Be gone and take your ugly bitch home with you!"

Well that was all Deborah needed to hear, and before Gabriel knew it the two women were fighting it out in his foyer, Deborah throwing man-licks and swinging Terrie by her hair as the white girl screamed and cried.

Moments later the music had stopped and Gabriel had an audience at the back door. Somebody grabbed hold of

Deborah as Gabriel held Shyne, and Della pushed her way inside and brushed Terrie off as she helped the girl off the floor where Deborah had dropped her.

"I'll slaughter that bitch!" Shyne roared. He was drunk as hell. He slurred his words and swung a wild punch, almost catching Gabriel on the side of the head as he lunged for Terrie. "Let her go, Mama! I'll lay the bitch out cold!"

Gabriel was embarrassed as he hustled Deborah and Shyne out the door and toward Deborah's car. He couldn't tell who had drunk the most between the two of them, and when Deborah climbed behind the wheel Gabriel figured she was holding her liquor much better than Shyne, so if they were going to have a chance at getting home without killing themselves or somebody else, he'd put his money on her.

Gabriel walked back into his house slowly, and the look on Michelle's face was one of sadness and disappointment. There was far more than that lurking on Della's face, and before she could open her mouth and let all of that poison fall out, Gabriel snatched Terrie and pushed her toward the door too.

"Just wait a damn minute," his mother protested as she tried to break Gabriel's hold on the girl and get between them. "Terrie came over here with *me*! You can't just throw her out like that! Her little girl is upstairs asleep in your house!"

Gabriel never broke his stride as he grabbed his mother under her arm and escorted her toward the front door as well. "Michelle," he called to his wife, his voice cold and grim. "Get that child and bring her outside to her mother." And then to Della he said quietly, "This is *my goddamn house,* Mama. And if I can put Shyne out I can damn sure put you and Terrie out too."

Gabriel sat up as the voice of a stewardess filled the cabin. They were about to land and he brought his seat back upright as instructed and made sure his seat belt was fastened. Della's head was lolled back on her headrest and she opened her eyes the moment he touched her arm.

"We're almost there, Mama," he said, then waited as she raised her seat back and composed herself. Della was quiet as the plane descended, and thirty minutes later as they sped toward Quincy Correctional Facility she still hadn't spoken more than a handful of words.

Gabriel saw a huddle of flickering lights as they approached the main gate, and it took him a moment to realize that what he was seeing was lit candles. Candles held high by the hundreds of death penalty opponents and supporters who had turned out to witness Shyne's execution. The press had already set up camp, and the stationary lights shone on the scores of picket signs being waved by people who chanted slogans like, "Killing People for ANY Reason Is Cruel and Inhumane" and "A Life for a Life."

"Come on, Mama," Gabriel said gently as their party was escorted by four prison guards to a side entrance away from the throngs of protestors. Della moved slowly and looked frightened, and Gabriel was shocked when he realized how aged his mother appeared. "We'll be safe inside," he assured her as they were led into the lobby of the death house.

Gabriel looked around and his chest went tight. It had been years since the last man was executed in the chamber upstairs, but he could still sense the aura of death in the air.

"Never," he muttered under his breath, the drab gray walls seeming to close in on him. All the metal bars, the guards, the desperate, dangerous men who sat in places like this day after day turning into animals . . . "Never," Gabriel told himself again. He had a lot of respect for men like Shyne. Men who had a whole lot more courage than he ever wanted to possess. Prison wasn't for him.

He'd die before he let somebody cuff him and drag him into a pissy little cell with some lifelong criminal. Shyne was the bigger man, Gabriel concluded as the guards led him and Della to a small visiting room where Shyne was waiting to receive them. Yeah, Gabriel thought guiltily at the first sight of his brother as he sat talking to the warden in the small cell, Shyne was definitely the better man too.

TICKTOCK

10 O'CLOCK

DEBORAH Three hours earlier, Deborah James had stepped into New York City's Port Authority wearing a blue rain poncho, jeans, and a pair of dirty Tims. It was only October, but an early winter ice storm had swept through the city and the cotton T-shirt Deborah wore under the plastic poncho had been no match for the bitter winter rain.

For Deborah, life was just as cold as the biting, frigid air. She was hungry as all hell and down to her last three Newport loosies. But with only a dollar forty-eight and a round-trip ticket to her name, she ignored her stomach and concentrated on finding the only bus that was heading toward Quincy for the night.

Moving fast, Deborah had pushed through the crowd on the busy platform breathing in exhaust fumes and cursing under her breath. She'd come real close to not making it to the bus station at all, and the thought that she might never see Shyne again scared the shit out of her. Deborah wasn't the type to let herself be trampled on, but she had swallowed her pride and gotten down on her hands and knees and begged Verlie's fat ass to loan her enough money to catch the bus upstate. Verlie had known it was going to be a long trip and that Deborah was dead broke, but the half-French Louisiana bitch was so cruel that she had agreed to take care of Deborah's bus fare but wouldn't budge on a dime more.

"How am I supposed to eat, Verlie? The bus don't leave from up there until two o'clock the next morning. What the hell am I supposed to eat all night and half the next day?"

Verlie had laughed, her painted lips gleaming and her devilish eyes glinting. "You still selling ass, ain't you, baby? Well, you carrying way more than one woman needs back there, sugar. Sell off enough to buy you a sandwich so you can eat on the bus, child. I'll put your ticket on my credit card," her stepmother had said in her grating, high-pitched voice, "but you gonna work off the whole damn bill before you leave out of here."

And Verlie hadn't been playing either. That lazy, toad-looking bitch had kept Deborah on her knees for three days straight hand washing everything from her funky-ass panty hose to a pile of musty, hundred-year-old quilts. Deborah's fingertips had shriveled and peeled, and the palms of her hands sprouted water-filled blisters, but she'd scrubbed all Verlie's shit without a mumble of complaint. Verlie could be dealt with later, Deborah had told herself. Right then the most important thing was getting that Greyhound ticket so she could get on that bus and upstate to see Shyne.

Almost four years had passed since Shyne had gotten busted for rape and murder, and for more than three of those years he'd been locked down on death row. Before his trial they'd had him locked away on Rikers, and even though she'd had to go way to Queens and then catch a dirty little bus to cross the bridge to the island, Deborah and Shyne shared a lot of history and she had been a true rider.

Deborah had still been working on her recovery back then, steady on her job and keeping herself clean. In fact, she'd still had her apartment too, and in between making daily meetings and running back and forth to see Shyne—then running back and forth to Family Court fighting her ex for visitation with their daughter—Deborah had been too busy to think about getting high.

Her family thought she was crazy to keep standing by Shyne after the kind of twisted crimes he'd committed, but Deborah let all their bullshit criticisms roll off her back. When Shyne was out on the streets doing good and had money falling out of all his pockets her people had been first on line holding out their hands to get as much as they could out of him. Now that he had taken a fall and was down and out and locked up where he couldn't get his hands around their necks they threw all kinds of shitty dirt on him seven days a week.

But Deborah *had* stood by her man. She was a dedicated wifey who rode hard with Shyne through thick and thin, and those twice-a-week visits to Rikers Island had been her way of showing her man that no matter how bad she'd stumbled during her testimony in that courtroom, her love was still righteous—even if her memory wasn't.

Deborah shuddered. So much had happened since the night she'd kicked Terrie's ass at Shug's barbeque. So much had been lost to her after that night, including her battle with crack cocaine. Shyne might have gone to jail, but Deborah had been imprisoned too, a victim of her own addictions. She had been rushing out of a drug house when she found out they were going to execute him.

"Yo, Dee!" A guy named Black Oscar had called to her from the doorway of a fish joint across the street. Deborah had been on an all-night mission in an abandoned apartment above a store on Sutter Avenue. She'd already smoked up her check and had come outside to hustle up enough money to go back upstairs and do it all over again.

She squinted across the street where Black Oscar stood leaning and swaying in the wind. Drunk or high, Black Oscar was one of the smartest people on the streets of Brooklyn, so when he waved her over Deborah put her mission on hold and crossed the street to hear what he had to say.

"You heard about your boy, right?"

He was talking about Shyne and Deborah knew it. She shivered and shook her head. Her high was fading fast, even though the crack stem in her hand was still warm.

"Nah." She raised her hand and shielded her blood-shot eyes from the morning sun. She nodded toward the dope house. "I been up in the trap all night."

Black Oscar delivered the news with all the solemnity he could muster. "Well, you know Shyne gave up all his appeals, right? Now that faggot-ass governor done set him a date. They gonna put him down next week. Your boy's number is up."

His words hit Deborah hard enough to blow her high straight into the wind. She took two steps back and staggered, fear creeping into her eyes as she bit down on her lip.

"How you know all that, Oscar?" Her voice was full of disbelief but her heart knew the whole truth. Shyne was really gonna die.

"I read the papers, sweetheart. I watch the damn news. I get my head bad, yeah, but I stay up on what's going with my people too. They gonna do him at midnight next Thursday, Dee. Sorry, baby, but your boy is done for. They about to put him down for a nice long dirt nap."

Black Oscar's words had been ringing in Deborah's ears as she climbed on the seven o'clock bus to Quincy, New York, and hurried down the aisle. Her stomach was sour from nerves as she stumbled past her fellow travelers and glanced briefly at a few: big mama with her orthopedic shoes sticking out in the aisle, two project-looking gangstas who were probably running drugs upstate to sell in white neighborhoods, and a young gum-popping girl with two kids who had "baby-mama-drama" written all over her face.

Deborah sat near the back of the bus and put her wet shoes up on the seat beside her. She was nervous. The day before she'd gotten a phone call from some warden who wanted to know if Shyne had a burn on his back. Why the fuck he needed to know that escaped her, but she'd told him the truth anyway. Deborah stared out the window. Her hands were cold and clammy as she pulled out a half-crushed box of Newport Kings and lit one.

She had only taken two or three pulls when the young chick with the baby swung her head around and mean mugged the shit out of her.

"There's no smoking on the goddamn bus!" The girl pointed to a sign mounted above the driver's head. "Didn't you see the sign when you got on here? It says no fucking smoking!" She turned back around, fanning her hands and popping junk. "People are so fucking stupid. They see kids on here and still don't have no respect."

Deborah nodded, not even riled. Yeah. Cool, bitch. She took another deep drag and clipped her cigarette, stomping the embers out on the floor as she put the remaining half back inside the box. Let the young chick talk, Deborah decided. As long as she kept talking from her seat, the girl was just another ass whipping for another day, but even with her mind so full of Shyne, if loudmouth got up and brought that noise to the back,

Deborah would have stuck her foot straight up the young girl's ass.

But the bus driver was standing outside the door collecting tickets, and since Deborah was on probation and sneaking her ass out of the city, she sat back and relaxed and hoped the young chick would too. Despite her temper, her addiction, and the lingering doubts that kept her getting high and losing sleep at night, Deborah could be a real smart chick when she wanted to be. Beating the girl up would only draw unwanted attention to herself, so if she had to go a few hours without a cigarette then she would, because there was nothing in the world that could stop her from getting upstate to see Shyne.

Deborah watched from her window seat as the bus driver helped riders push suitcases and baby strollers into the cargo compartment of the bus. Jails made her nervous no matter which side of the bars she was on, and while she was anxious and exhausted to the bone, she was also scared to close her eyes. She stared at the people who were still walking around on the platform and tried to figure out where the hell they were going and what kind of fucked-up shit they'd done in life that had led them to a Greyhound station on a bitter cold night in October.

For her, almost every bitter cold night in her life had come down to Shyne.

She'd started fooling around with him when she was seventeen and hot as hell.

Shyne had been about twenty back then. He spent a lot of time with some thugs who took bets on a garage full of vicious pit bulls, and Verlie had nearly peed when she found out Shyne was involved in illegal dogfighting.

"You ain't got a bit of taste. That boy ain't shit, ain't never gonna be shit," Deborah's father had warned. Truth be told, Shyne had been a little too big and too black for Deborah's taste too, plus he ran with a crew of hoods who robbed and stole and brought terror down on the neighborhood, which wasn't cute at all, but the moment those words left her father's mouth Deborah had started liking Shyne real fine and wanting him even more.

"Don't worry about me," she'd told the old man and shook her hips as she walked away. Deborah had been a change-of-life baby and her mother had died when she was ten. The fat, chicken-looking lump sitting beside her father was his second wife, Verlie, who was also Deborah's mother's younger sister and Deborah's aunt. "No matter how bad I pick them," she'd said, smirking over her shoulder at her aunt, "I can still pick 'em ten times better than *that.*"

Before Deborah knew it she was hooked on Shyne. She was his lover, his ride or die, his partner in crime, and his friend to the end. There was nothing she wouldn't do for him, and over the years she'd proven that. She was the Bonnie to his Clyde. When she ran away from her father's house Shyne was living in some hole in the wall off Saratoga Avenue. The little room was dark and musty, with no water and no bathroom, but she'd kept it nice and neat and as long as Shyne was laying there next to her all night, it was their castle. Whatever Shyne was into, Deborah was into it too. She'd spent some time in jail for helping him rob a drug dealer, and when the cops caught her and Shyne got away, Deborah kept her mouth closed and did her six months without a single complaint because she knew her man would have done the same thing for her.

But as tight as they were, there was another side to Shyne that Deborah had learned to fear. Shyne had a reputation for viciousness on the streets, and because of his size and his temper he commanded a lot of respect. Shyne could be a moody ass, and sometimes when he got quiet he got nasty. But when he got drunk he was downright dangerous and Deborah learned to stay out of his way when he isolated himself with a bottle. They had been together for almost a year when Deborah found out just how cold and dangerous Shyne could be, but by that time they were steady drinking and snorting and party-ing all over Brooklyn, and Deborah had already estab-lished herself as the bling on Shyne's arm.

Coming from the swamps of Louisiana Deborah's family was part Cajun, and just like the rest of her kinfolk Deborah could drink all night and still stand up straight without a lean or a wobble. But Shyne was the kind of man who just didn't need to flirt with alcohol because a couple of drinks were never enough, and it only took a little bit to bring out the worst in him. Deborah found out how true this was when he got drunk then came up in her father's house and tore the door off the hinges.

"Bitch," he breathed, standing in the doorway with both hands high on the busted frame. "You been going through my shit?"

They'd been staying with her father for about a month, and Deborah was on her hands and knees sorting the laundry; throwing the white clothes in one pile and the colored clothes in another. She'd just picked up a pair of his pants and pulled the leg right side out, and was going through his pockets to make sure he hadn't left any tissue or paper or nothing that might get washed by mistake.

Shyne had been drinking heavily and Deborah could smell the Hennessy on his breath from where he stood. He stomped into the room sweating and looking crazy as hell, and Deborah saw something that looked like pure hatred flash in his unfocused eyes.

"Get your fuckin' hands out my pockets, bitch."

Deborah could sense the danger rising in him and she tried to do him the way she used to do her father when he went on one of drunken tirades.

"Man, sit your ass down. Nobody was in your pockets, goddammit. I'm in here washing your nasty clothes, so don't come talking no shit to me. Now what you gonna do about my damn front door you just busted down?"

"Fuck your door!" Shyne raged. "Get the fuck outta my shit!"

They were alone in the apartment and Deborah kept up her brave, aggressive front although she wondered if Shyne was too far drunk for her strategy to work.

"Look, niggah." Her voice was full of authority as she tried to psych Shyne's drunk ass into backing down. "This is *my* damn daddy's place, remember? You don't come up in here talking to me any old kinda way in *my* damn place, ya know?"

The next thing Deborah knew she was stretched out in the pile of laundry seeing black. She touched the side of her face where her temple was swelling fast and her vision was going as well.

"You hit me . . ."

That one must have been a love tap because the real punches came next.

They flurried down on her head and back and there was no stopping him as he beat her like she'd been in his pockets stealing his cash.

All Deborah knew was to fight back. She grabbed him around his feet and sank her teeth into his ankle. When he kicked her off she grabbed at him and bit down again.

"Bitch! Quit biting me!" Shyne yelled.

He kicked her off and Deborah slid on her butt and ended up pressed against the wall. Shyne climbed on top of her, squeezing her by the throat while unbuckling his pants. He grabbed at her skirt and she tried to kick him in the crotch but missed. He let go of her neck as she gasped for air, and used his knees and hands to hold her legs apart while he rammed himself into her.

"What the hell you doing, Shyne?"

Deborah fought from the floor, surprised as hell. She always gave him plenty of ass. Ass coming out of ass. There was no reason for him to take it from her.

"I bet you won't bite me again, now will you, bitch?" Shyne's voice came out raspy as he slammed into her over and over again.

Deborah couldn't answer, and when he was finished he gave one more good thrust then got up and shook himself off. She thought it was over, but the moment he pulled up his pants a tan-colored Tim caught her right under her chin.

"Next time you put your hands in my pockets I'll kill you."

With sobriety came amnesia with Shyne, and he didn't remember a minute of it the next day. He didn't remember a thing he'd said or a thing he had done.

"Boo why you saying stuff like that?" he pleaded as he cradled her in his big arms and held a washcloth filled with ice against the lump he'd kicked up on the side of her face. "Why would I fight you and steal a piece of ass from you, girl? You like giving it to me just as much as I like getting it. Now tell me what really happened, Dee. And tell me the truth too."

All Deborah knew as she repeated exactly what he'd done to her one more time is that Shyne high on weed and maybe a little blow was one thing. But Shyne drunk on liquor was something else. Something she didn't ever want to be around again if she could help it.

There were other dark spots in Shyne's life that not even the light of her love could penetrate, but it wasn't until he took her to his mother's crib that Deborah began to understand why his head could be so messed up at times.

"Deb, this is my brother, Shug. Shug, this my girl, Deb. The one I told you about."

Deborah had stood there looking up at a version of her man that made her stop in her tracks. He was almost like Shyne, but different. They had the same tall, muscular build, the same smooth dark skin, dimples, and a real similar smile. But that's where it ended.

Deborah stared into Shug's brown eyes and saw something in them that wasn't in Shyne's. Instead of the raw, rugged street look that her man projected, there was a powerful aura of confidence flowing from his brother, and even before Shug opened his mouth to greet her, Deborah knew their games were from the opposite ends of the track.

And she was right. Shug was educated and had been to college somewhere out on Long Island. Shyne was street smart and had learned his life lessons thumping in the trenches with the best the hood had to offer.

But they were close and Deborah could see it right away. Like they shared a lot of secrets that nobody else knew about. Shyne had told her that when he was a kid he'd had to fight for almost everything he got. If that was true, it sure hadn't been because of Shug. It was easy to tell that what these brothers shared together ran equally in both directions.

Deborah found herself fascinated by Shug, and even though he probably thought she was a piece of regular old project trash, he went out of his way to be nice to her. Now, Shug might have been cool, but that damn mama they had was on some serious shit. Della Blackwood had hated Deborah on sight. Her eyes had raked the girl up and down, then she'd shaken her head like Shyne was an alley cat who had dragged a little ghetto mouse through her door.

She wouldn't even speak when they were introduced, and when Deborah said hi and held out her hand, Della had ignored her and turned to Shyne instead.

"Is this the heffah you been running the streets with? Is she the best you could find?"

"Don't hold me back!" Deborah had yelled, pulling away from Shyne and snatching off her earrings.

Deborah got mad all over again just thinking about that day. Della had called her black and ugly and told Shyne to make sure he didn't bring no nappy-headed tar babies around her house, and she'd meant it too.

Deborah had been so mad she wanted to cry. His mama didn't know her like that! She would have whipped Della's ass if she could have gotten to her, but Shyne had held her back while Shug tried to shush Della.

"Your mama got a problem," Deborah told him. "How

she gonna go off like that when she don't know nothing about me?"

Shyne had laughed it off, but Deborah had seen the pain hiding deep in his eyes. "It ain't you she has the problem with, baby. It's me."

Deborah had kept her distance from Della after that, and for the next few years they only bumped into each other occasionally, and there was absolutely no love lost between them when they did.

To say that Deborah and Shyne went through some insane things together over the next five years or so wouldn't be doing either of them a bit of justice. They'd gotten down for each other and done it all. But one thing that Deborah and Shyne hadn't done together was make a baby.

Deborah sighed as she looked out the window and thought about her daughter. Not all of her years with Shyne had been good years. There were a couple of days when she could have killed his ass. Like the time she was deep in her addiction and he left her for that white girl. Terrie. The same girl he was sitting on death row for killing right now. Shyne had been on parole and had picked up a small-time job washing cars just to keep his parole officer happy. The guy was still after him though, and even though Shyne reported for all his appointments and worked steady, every time they looked up the guy was coming by the house to check shit out. But Deborah had been getting high in the apartment and Shyne had a problem with it.

"I can see you smoking maybe a little weed," Shyne told Deborah one night after his parole officer showed up out of the blue and almost caught her smoking crack right in the kitchen. "But those fish scales should be off-limits, girl. If that honkie finds out there's drugs in the crib he's gonna violate my ass and send me straight back to jail."

It was impossible for Deborah to just up and turn her crack jones off just like that, so of course she kept smoking every chance she got. And after all the dirty shit Deborah had done with him and for him, Shyne had caught her puffing one time too many and tossed her straight into the trash can. No matter how bad she begged and cried, he had walked out of her life at a time when she needed him most.

You couldn't tell Deborah she wouldn't die without Shyne because she really thought she would. But somebody had told her there was always a reason for whatever happened in life, and losing Shyne had actually allowed Deborah to find a sense of her own self and to find a love that was a million times bigger than the one she'd shared with him.

She had been groveling at the bottom of the barrel when Shyne walked out, and there was really not much lower she could go. After crying for three solid days and halfheartedly sliding a razor blade across her wrist, Deborah had allowed a girlfriend to take her to a rehab center in Westchester County, and sixty days later she had gained seventeen pounds and cleared away some of the fog in her head.

It was hard going back to Brooklyn clean and sober and seeing the same people, the same sights, and walking down the same streets, but Deborah had done it. She got a job at a clothing store on Pitkin Avenue and turned her back when her ex-friends called to her from stoops and doorways and offered to share their rocks.

While working on Pitkin, Deborah met a guy in a record shop, fucked him a few times, and got pregnant. She could have jazzed the story up and pretended they'd been in some kind of deep-ass love affair or something, but that's just not how it happened and Deborah didn't have the energy to make it seem any other way. So on a warm spring day in April, Deborah officially became a baby mama. Her daughter Samitra was born cute and healthy and the moment Deborah saw her, she fell in love.

She'd moved back in with her father and Verlie and loved her baby girl with a heart that was a million times more giving than it had been when she was running around with Shyne. Staring into Samitra's huge brown eyes, Deborah vowed she was going to build a good life for her daughter and get them both out of the hood.

But she didn't. By the time Samitra was three Deborah had relapsed and was back out on the streets again. The courts had awarded custody of the child to her father, and it took an accident to bring Deborah back to her senses.

It was right before Samitra's fourth birthday, and fate had helped Deborah get clean again. She was running across Linden Boulevard to catch a trick when she found herself tumbling across the hood of a green Toyota, every bone in her body popping and screaming with pain. She hit the ground hard and was knocked out, and when she woke up she was in the emergency room at Kings County Hospital with a broken collarbone and a dislocated hip.

For the next few weeks she'd used a cane to get around, but she still couldn't carry anything in her right arm. She had just gotten home from a physical therapy appointment when she looked up and saw Shyne walking toward her.

"How you doing, stranger?" she called to him as she struggled to get out of a taxi near her apartment. Shyne had gotten locked up on a parole violation six months after Deborah had Samitra, and even though they weren't together she'd been real good about keeping in touch and sending him baby pictures until the pipe grabbed her and she started using again.

"My neighbor was supposed to come down and meet the cab and help me on the stairs, but you know how that is. Can you get me up there?"

Shyne had paid for her taxi and carried her like a baby upstairs to her third-floor apartment, and Deborah had never been happier to see anybody in her life. He kept her company that night and one thing led to another, but she could tell things weren't all the way right between them.

"You clean?" he asked, and Deborah was disappointed that he couldn't tell by the way she looked. Yeah, he had a right to ask, but there were a couple of questions Deborah had for him too. For one thing, was he still fucking with Terrie? Deborah's shoulder might've been sore and her hip out of joint, but she'd still rode his ass like he was a brand-new dirt bike and he'd come long and hard and didn't let her go for at least fifteen minutes afterward.

"Stay with me," Deborah begged him. "I'm here by myself and I'm lonely. Samitra comes over every other weekend, but besides that I'm by myself." Deborah was lucky to have a roof over her head and she knew it. Samitra's father had set her up in a one-bedroom apartment so she would have someplace to keep her daughter on the weekends because he was married to a West Indian woman who refused to let Deborah in her house.

It wasn't until after Shyne moved in with her that Deborah found out how crazy Terrie was. She had a daughter who was a little younger than Samitra, and once Shyne came back to Deborah, Terrie went to war on his ass. More than once Shyne was forced to smack her ass up and put her in check.

And that was the part of all this that made Deborah's heart pound and kept her up shaking and sweating at night. Shyne had been with her that night, three years earlier, when Terrie and her little girl were killed. Deborah couldn't stand the girl, but the thought of what Terrie and her small daughter must have suffered through ate away at her heart. The cops had kept some of the worst details about the crime out of the papers, but with a black man accused of killing a white woman and her child, everybody in New York City knew exactly what Shyne had supposedly done to that baby.

Deborah had been subpoenaed as a defense witness and had sat through the trial in a state of turmoil. She couldn't stop shaking up on that witness stand as all those people watched her with condemnation in their eyes. A big black nigger like Shyne had stuck his dick inside of a white baby, and Deborah had never seen so many pissed-off white people in her life. They were lined up outside the courthouse each morning when she walked up, calling her nasty names and throwing insults left and right. You would have thought she was the one on trial instead of Shyne.

And the prosecutor was no better. She was a washed-out-looking white chick who wrecked shit in the courtroom. Not only was she sharp, you could tell she'd done her homework and everybody else's. She never seemed to ask a question unless she already knew the answer, and the woman took down Shyne's defense team with the power of forty bulls. She hadn't left a single stone unturned in her prosecution, and every one of her ducks was lined up in a row.

Deborah had watched the way Janet Lovitz sweated and got red in the face when she was presenting her evidence to the jury. She heard the way her voice rose and got all squeaky as she talked about how big and strong Shyne was, and how much damage he'd inflicted on poor little Arielle. The woman was so damned good at her job that Deborah found herself boo-hooing like hell over that dead baby. And the way Janet glared at Shyne, and

Shug, and even at Della with such hatred and disgust in her eyes made Deborah think her prosecution of the case bordered on something personal.

Deborah had gotten the shitty eye on the stand too. She was from the hood, and she knew when a chick was stepping to her with hostility, and Janet definitely was trying to throw some salt in Deborah's Kool-Aid. Ordinarily, Deborah would have told a bitch like Janet something clever, but this wasn't the time or the place, so she concentrated on answering the questions without making things any worse for Shyne than they already were.

Yes, she looked right in Janet's eyes and admitted there had been some words between her and Shyne's mother during the barbeque. And hell yeah she'd swung on the deceased, and if Shyne hadn't stepped between them she would have flown Terrie's blond head against the wall. The problem was, Terrie had been calling her names and laughing at her. Every time she'd looked up Terrie and Della had been covering their mouths and pointing at her, and if Shyne hadn't gotten drunk and started slapping Terrie around, it would have been Deborah and Terrie going at it full force for sure.

When did she realize the situation had gotten out of hand? From the moment Shyne took his first drink. Liquor and Isaiah Blackwood just did not mix, and when he was dipping in those cups he was nothing nice and everybody in the joint could vouch for that.

Had she seen Arielle Mills on the night in question? Yes, earlier in the day. Deborah couldn't stand the sight of Terrie, but she had to admit that Arielle was a sweet baby, and for some reason the little girl couldn't stay away from her.

"Miss Debbah," Arielle would always say, buttering Deborah up. "You look niiiice. Can I play with Meetra?"

How the hell was Deborah supposed to say no? She couldn't stand Terrie's ass, but that baby of hers was like a cute little honeybee that worked herself into everybody's heart, and even Deborah wasn't immune.

And this is what had brought her full circle with her thoughts and made her heart slam into her throat. The autopsy photos showed how Arielle had been busted wide open. The coroner's report said she was bloody and broken up but still alive when she was thrown in that yard with all those vicious dogs. They'd bitten right through her soft little neck. One of her arms had been torn off, and the other one was gnawed down to the bone.

If, Deborah demanded of herself, just *if* Shyne was capable of sticking his big dick into some sweet little three-year-old white girl, did that mean he could stick it into a sweet little four-year-old black girl too?

Deborah had freaked out at the sight of the gruesome crime scene and autopsy photos. She'd ducked her head and shut her eyes as they loomed large on a screen, then ran screaming from the courtroom as a picture of Arielle's bloody, gaped legs and naked bruised body assaulted her and burned itself in her memory.

Later, after she'd smoked a cigarette and bummed a few sips of wine from a guy around the corner from the courthouse, Deborah was able to return to the stand and resume her testimony. Yeah, she was a bad bitch from the projects and would fight a full-grown man in a minute, but she'd cried like a baby as she told the jury how Shyne had been so drunk the night of Terrie and Arielle's murder that she'd practically had to drag his big heavy ass into her room and put him in the bed. Sure, she'd been pretty well toasted that night herself, but she had testified to how Shyne had been so wasted that he'd snored loud and hard throughout the night and that it was her who had told him about Terrie's murder when he finally opened his eyes sometime the next afternoon.

Deborah had sworn to these things with her right hand up to God, and dammit every single word she had said was true. But what Deborah didn't tell the jury was that there were a few pieces of the puzzle that just didn't fit, even in her mind. Yeah, Shyne was a big man who snored like a lawn mower, and it was the absence of this sound, the pure silence that had awakened her in the middle of the night.

It had been close to 4 a.m. when Deborah rolled over in bed looking for him. She'd gotten up, thinking Shyne might be in the bathroom, but the door was open and the light was off. It was on her way back to bed that Deborah noticed something wasn't right. She peered through her small railcar-shaped apartment and almost caught a fever when she saw that her front door was open and a glow from the streetlight outside was spilling in through the crack.

There wasn't a bit of fear in her as she marched over to the door and yanked it open. No, the fear would come much later. She remembered thinking Shyne must have bumped his head walking out of her house in the middle of the night. There had to be Terrie or some other bitch involved because Shyne damn sure hadn't gotten up out the bed to go chasing after no man.

Deborah had looked up and down the street, fuming. A cool breeze blew into the apartment and pressed her gown against her naked body. A yellow and red sign was still lit at Charlies, a chicken and rib joint less than two blocks away, and Deborah knew they wouldn't stop serving the club hoppers until the sun came up and shut the joint down.

She was standing on her front stoop mad as hell when she saw him. Lumbering down the block with his shirt off and his pants low around his waist.

This motherfucker . . . Deborah thought, but when she saw what was in his hands her anger had dissipated into the cool morning air.

"Why the hell," she called down when he was close enough to hear, "you go out here and leave my damn door wide open! We got plenty of food right up in here. You couldn't have been that damn hungry." She peered down at his Styrofoam plate of food. "You ate all those wings and didn't save me none?"

Shyne had climbed the stairs, and with his fingers coated hot sauce red he'd shrugged Deborah away, turning his body to shield his plate.

"Gimme one," Deborah had said, happy her man was back and hadn't been out fucking no other bitches, especially white ones. "Didn't your raggedy mama ever teach you how to share?"

"Nah, she didn't," Shyne had grumbled, blocking his plate as he stumbled into the apartment.

"Well she should have!" Deborah yelled at his wide, strong back. "That bitch was sleeping on the job, baby.

She was straight sleeping, ya hear? And where the hell is your shirt, Shyne? Damn, Terrie scratched the shit outta your neck! Don't take that chicken in my room, I mean that shit. Your mama should have taught you not to eat in people's beds too. Damn! Was that bitch Della high or drunk when she was supposed to be raising y'all? She was sleep, I'm telling you. Sleep!"

And minutes later, so was Shyne. Asleep in her bed, hugging a plate of hot wings and once again snoring like a lawn mower.

They were nearing the prison and Deborah shifted in her seat, trying to ease her aching hip. It was pitch-black outside except for an occasional set of headlights and the intermittent road reflectors, and Deborah wondered if Shyne would ever see the sun again.

The trauma of his trial still haunted her. For four days there had been scores of people crying in the courtroom. Sometimes loud and emotional, but there had also been that real quiet crying too. The kind where you could tell they were paying attention to everything going on around them, but the tears were just leaking from their eyes and running down their faces like water. Like they didn't even realize the tears were there.

Deborah couldn't even lie. She had cried then, and she still cried now. Except there was guilt mixed in with her grief, and it was this guilt that had sent her running back out into the streets for drugs and kept her crying long into the night.

Shyne's mama had completely flipped during the trial. It had been crazy watching the way she sat on the bench all hugged up with Terrie's family. She had mean mugged Shyne like he was somebody else's child, and the message on her face for the whole world to see was nothing nice.

I'll be damned, Deborah had thought as she watched Della, *if I give these judgmental motherfuckers that kind of satisfaction!* Della was embarrassed, that's all. Ashamed that Shyne was her child and desperate to make these crackers think she was a good little house nigger who had somehow slipped up and shit out a field slave.

But as much as Deborah despised Della, guilt and doubt were crippling her own game too. She was just too damn defiant to show it. She'd turned the situation over and over in her head for almost four years, but she still couldn't come up with enough to be absolutely sure.

Something had gone down right after Deborah's accident that still tormented her today. It was a warm afternoon in May and the Handi-Van had just dropped her off from her physical therapy appointment. Deborah was walking pretty good now and could get up and down the stairs without much trouble.

It was the Friday before Memorial Day and she had Samitra for the long weekend. Deborah had left her and Shyne outside playing handball against the building before her appointment, and when she got back home and walked into the apartment the first thing she heard was the sound of running water. She moved toward the half-opened door of the bathroom and froze.

"Turn around," she heard Shyne say. He was on his knees by the bathtub where Samitra was naked, standing in several inches of soapy water.

Deborah watched as Shyne dragged the bubbly rag across her little girl's shoulders and ran it down her arms. She gasped at the sight of Samitra's slender, soapy neck. The curve of her glistening back, and the small mound of her baby butt that already held the assurances of a future brick house.

"What you doing?" Deborah blurted and barged into the bathroom. She snatched Samitra by one arm and lifted her dripping out of the tub.

Shyne looked up at her, puzzled. "What the hell do it look like I'm doing? I'm giving her a bath."

"Why you giving her a bath? You ain't never gave her one before. Plus, she already had one this morning."

"We was out there playing in the grass, Deb. She wanted to go up the street and roll down that hill, so we did. But then she started itching and scratching and shit and there was welts coming up on her." He shrugged. "I brought her back home and figured I should wash the grass off her, that's all. Shug used to get like that around grass when we was little kids, and that's what my mother used to do for him."

The moment of tension had passed quickly, and Deborah had felt sorry for her baby girl when she dried Samitra off and saw all the hivelike welts on her arms and legs. She had rubbed her down with Benadryl and forgotten about the whole thing until the day little Arielle's brutalized body was found.

Immediately, Deborah had gone back to that scene in the bathroom, and she battled with herself over what she thought she might have seen that day. *Trust your instincts,* a small voice inside her warned, but she smacked that thought away real quick. *You're a fucking crackhead, Deborah!* she chastised herself. *Your instincts usually lead you straight to a pipe!*

But still . . . the question had lingered on her mind and never really died. Was Shyne simply soaping Samitra's back, or was he *rubbing* her baby . . . the way it looked when she'd walked in?

As the Greyhound bus rolled into the town of Quincy, Deborah still didn't know. There was no way to be sure for real, for real. But there was one thing that Deborah did know. Not long after she caught Shyne bathing her daughter, Samitra started refusing to spend any time at all with Deborah, and her father damn sure didn't force her to.

"Why, Samitra?" Deborah had begged her daughter over the phone. "Mommy loves you, baby! Mommy wants to see you. I'll come see you at Daddy's house if you want me to. Just ask him!"

But no matter what Deborah said, Samitra pushed her away, cut her off, and her daughter's rejection was just what Deborah needed to send her back out on the streets again, searching for that rock. She blamed herself for not being a good enough mother, for smoking crack when she was pregnant with Samitra, and for running the streets during the early days of her daughter's life when she should have been at home bonding with her child.

It wasn't until later, when Shyne was arrested for raping and killing Arielle, that the silent rebuke from her own four-year-old little girl came flooding back to

Deborah's heart. *What if it wasn't about me,* she thought, horrified down to her bones. What if Samitra had stopped coming to see her because of Shyne? Deborah almost rejoiced. Maybe it wasn't even me! Maybe I wasn't such a loser after all!

Did he wash her? *Or did he touch her?*

Deborah would probably never know. Her ex had moved back to Jamaica two years ago, taking Samitra with him. Deborah knew that her baby was probably forever out of her reach, but somehow it didn't hurt as bad when she hung that noose around Shyne's neck instead of around her own.

She loved Shyne. She loved that man all down in her bones. And yeah, blaming him for the loss of her daughter was damn hard to do.

But it was a whole lot easier than blaming herself.

TICKTOCK
11 O'CLOCK

VIRGIL Virgil Banks lit a cigarette and gazed out of a window on the second floor of the death house. He hadn't slept in more than twenty-four hours, and his hands shook as he pressed the Newport Light to his lips. The courtyard below was chaotic and lit with activity. A flood of New Yorkers, mostly white and mad as hell, had crammed through the gates and stood behind the police barricade waiting in anticipation of one great thing: revenge.

Death penalty advocates and their opponents had been gathering in the cold for hours, singing and praying up a storm. Just a high-profile circus show, Virgil thought, by a bunch of bleeding hearts who would rally around a fucking taco if you poured enough sauce on it.

Portable generators powered up lighting systems, and television crews maneuvered their cameras and audio wiring to get the best possible vantage points of the pre-execution rally. Virgil was almost drunk with exhaustion and disappointment as he watched the happenings with a worried frown creasing his face. Protests were chanted, fists were pumped, and boldly lettered picket signs were clenched in self-righteous hands. He squinted to make out some of the slogans on the signs: THOU SHALL NOT KILL AND LIVE AFTER IT! and ROT IN HELL CHILD MURDERER!

They were like wild dogs out there. Snapping and drooling and whining for a chunk of Isaiah Blackwood's ass. All of New York City had been hyped for weeks, anticipating this day, and every ten minutes a broadcaster would stare into a news camera and announce the time remaining on the execution clock like he was counting down the ball at Times Square on New Year's Eve.

Virgil shook his head and took a deep draw from his cigarette. He'd been on the phone for three days straight. First with the prosecuting DA, then with Blackwood's girlfriend, and finally with the governor. Nothing he'd tried had worked, and the swarm of people chanting below him was proof of that.

He crushed out the cigarette and rubbed his burning eyes. The local police were out in full force, and minutes ago they'd completely blocked off traffic at the main road. Virgil could understand the bloodlust. What Terrie and Arielle Mills had gone through was enough to keep every parent in the state of New York watching their kids like a bunch of hawks. Socking it to Isaiah Blackwood would give them permission to sleep nice and deep tonight. Shit, it would probably give them a few pleasant dreams as well.

As Virgil watched the crowd, he was filled with a sense of dread that burned ever deep. Why me? Why now? He'd asked himself those questions countless times over the past three days. To the rest of the world Isaiah Blackwood was just another convict. One less darkie out there on the streets to menace society. Virgil frowned and lit another cigarette. Now that executions were back on, brothers were going to start dropping like flies in every prison in the state.

It wasn't that Virgil felt any kind of sympathy for these fools, it was more like he was ashamed. He'd heard every story in the book during his twenty-two years of working in the correctional system, and even though most inmates swore they were innocent down to their dying breaths, nobody told a lie more convincingly than a man behind bars.

Virgil had started out as a prison guard at Rikers Island and then worked himself up to a position as warden. Over the years he'd developed a sixth sense about convicts, and when he looked into their eyes and listened to their bullshit stories, nine out of ten times he could see either the truth living in their eyes, or the lie before it left their lips.

And that's exactly how it was with Isaiah Blackwood.

It was funny how life changed on you. When Virgil was a kid, he wanted to be a lawyer so that he could fight for black men everywhere and liberate his brothers from social oppression and legal bondage. But the older he got and the more senseless shit he saw in his own community, it wasn't hard to see that most of his kinfolk were exactly where they belonged. Locked the hell up, instead of roaming the streets and free to creep through his windows and rob him at gunpoint every night.

Shit, better them than me, Virgil had learned to say. Sharing the same skin color oftentimes didn't count for a damn thing. *All my skin folks ain't my kinfolks* had become his mantra, because in his line of work he ran across countless black men that he couldn't even begin to identify with. The worst of those cats couldn't even be identified with the human race.

Which brought him back to his inmate Isaiah Blackwood and the brutal crime he was about to be executed for. He'd first met Blackwood back in the early days when he was an up-and-coming corrections officer working the tiers on Rikers Island. He'd finished his training and gotten his assignment, but it was a dangerous time to be coming on at that prison. There'd been a lot of static between Blacks and Hispanics, and a group of Mexicans had been going crazy over the gang rape, murder, and mutilation of one of their members.

After all these years Virgil still burned at the memory. When hopeless convicts went to war, no man was safe. It was lockup time late one night, and as he walked through the cell block on an inspection, a crazy Mexican inmate had rushed him from behind and pressed a shank into his throat. It was Blackwood who had saved his life that night. The inmate had caught Virgil off guard, and he had him pretty good. The shank was deep in his neck and blood was running down his shirt as Virgil struggled to call for backup and stop the guy from killing him at the same time.

While all the other inmates clapped and cheered and urged the Mexican to finish him off, Blackwood, a huge, bull-built young man, had thrown himself into the mix for no reason at all. Blood had been pouring from Virgil's throat when Blackwood stepped up and snatched the Mexican's knife hand and snapped it back until it cracked. Virgil had grunted with relief as Blackwood twisted the guy's arm so hard his shoulder popped out of joint, then proceeded to beat the shit out of him until Virgil's backup team arrived and saved the kid's life.

Virgil knew he owed his life to Blackwood, but when he approached him a few days later and asked him why he had put his prison rep on the line to save a guard, Blackwood had just shrugged.

"Why not?" he'd answered simply. "He jumped on you from behind. What kind of man could dig that?"

That had been more than twenty years ago, but Virgil had never forgotten it. He'd watched Blackwood for the rest of his bid on Rikers, but he had never managed to figure the man out. He'd been busted for possession of drugs, and no doubt he was guilty as hell, but even though the man was nothing more than a street hustler who deserved every day they slapped him with, Virgil had seen something in Blackwood that intrigued and impressed him too. The man had saved his life, and Virgil owed him. And that's why, years later when they crossed paths again and it was Virgil's opportunity to dole out a solid, he repaid Blackwood's favor the best way he knew how, a decision he would live to regret for the rest of his life.

Virgil had been born in a small dirt-road town called Coffee, Mississippi, to James and Virginia Banks, a gardener and a maid. Times were hard and money was short, and when James Banks took a job cleaning public toilets on Friday and Saturday nights, fifteen-year-old Virgil went with him.

It was dirty work but James and Virgil did it without complaint. Father and son worked side by side, toiling in the filth that strangers left behind. Coffee was a hick town, and Virgil's parents ate little, lived small, and scraped together every penny they could to get Virgil the things he needed to survive. When his classmates found out where he worked on the weekends, they teased him and called him shithead and pinched their noses when he walked by.

"Cleaning other people's shit," James Banks told his son when Virgil came home and said he was thinking of leaving school, "is what uneducated black men have to do to put food on the table. You take your ass back up to that school and get what you need. Let them rednecks laugh. One day you'll be laughing the loudest."

Coffee had its share of racial tensions and it wasn't unusual for black youngsters to find themselves caught in a run-in with the law. Benny Belford, the chief of police, was a bigot with five rowdy sons, and Virgil and his friends had spent their high school years ducking the Belford brothers and trying to stay out the way of their father's billy club.

During the summer after junior year of high school, Virgil and his best friend Hank Greenfield found themselves cornered by the Belford boys at the local movie theater. Hank was a tall, athletic kid whose good looks and easy charm made him popular with adults and kids alike in the black bottoms of Coffee. He too was going into his senior year and had already been promised a full basketball scholarship to UNC when he bested Jerry Belford in a game of one-on-one and all hell broke loose.

The game had been played in Coffee's largest public park, and some said Hank and Virgil were a couple of damn fools for stepping foot in the white folks' territory from the jump. But Virgil hadn't seen it that way. Five days a week his mother scrubbed floors and he and his father scrubbed shitters on the weekends. He and Hank had just as much right to walk on a public basketball court as anyone else in Coffee. Maybe even more.

The game had started out badly, with Hank getting fouled left and right. Jerry was a big kid, tall but soft. He threw his weight around and played dirty like a mother. Hank just grinned and took it, absorbing elbows in the gut, deliberate stomps on his heels, and accidental slaps upside the head whenever Jerry went up for a pack.

"All right, now." Hank grinned, taunting Jerry. A crowd of teenagers had formed and Jerry's brothers were taking bets and egging him on. "Smash that fuckin' monkey!" they hollered, and Jerry nodded and lowered his shoulder, then barreled into Hank and threw him to the ground.

"Twelve–six," Hank said, climbing to his feet with a good-natured smile. "You whipping me, man. We oughtta be playing football you so good with your shoulders, Jerry."

Virgil knew Hank had skills, and at a certain point he hoped his boy had some sense too. They were surrounded by white kids who wanted to see some black ass get whipped, and Virgil knew the situation was pretty critical. If Hank lost, they'd probably get their asses kicked all the way out the park. If Hank won, they'd probably die trying to get out the park. Either way there was going to be trouble, and Virgil stood on the sidelines screaming for Hank to bust that motherfucker up.

Later, Virgil would come to realize that it wasn't just that Hank had beaten Jerry's ass on the court that day. Hank had humiliated the white boy, and in the presence of about thirty of his friends. Getting out of that park without getting hurt was damn near impossible, and Hank pretty much sealed their fate during the final five minutes of the game.

"Eighteen–six," Hank shouted, then stepped aside and allowed Jerry to score an easy layup. "Point game!" Hank screamed, and then like a Dr. J–Magic Johnson–Michael Jordan clone, he proceeded to bust Jerry's ass and talk a mountain of shit while doing so.

"You soft!" Hank shouted, pushing off Jerry with his butt and spinning around for a dunk. He buzzed all over that court, dizzying Jerry with his speed and making gravity-defying moves that were so amazing that even the white boys screamed in awe. Jerry was sweating and growling as he got crossed over in rapid succession and tripped on his own feet.

Hank scored fourteen straight points, and the score was tied at point game. He scored the final point by zipping past Jerry and completing a hang-in-the-air gliding move that seemed like it left him suspended over the basket for about fifteen seconds. The Belford boys were on the court before the ball went through the net, and Hank fell into a pit of swinging white fists as he landed off his shot.

Virgil leaped over bodies trying to get to his boy.

He fought his way into the middle of the court where Hank was getting the shit stomped out of him by the Belford boys. He charged into the fray, giving Hank a chance to jump to his feet, and the two of them fought back like wild animals as the white boys closed in on them.

They were getting their asses kicked something awful when Virgil heard a sound that was better than sweet music in his ears. Blood was running from Hank's forehead and Virgil's left eye was already swollen shut. "Police," he managed to mutter, as they fought a fight that they were losing badly. Hope surged in him and he managed to swing a few blows as feet connected with his chin, groin, and back. If they could hold on long enough for the police to get out their cars and scatter the white boys, they might just live. But just as the crowd parted and blue bodies came into view, Virgil heard a loud crack. The crowd froze and Hank dropped like a tree. A yell of disbelief tore from Virgil's throat as the cops beat the shit out of his friend. Their billy clubs rose and fell without mercy, blood flying from Hank's forehead and splashing in arcs through the air.

Moments later they turned on Virgil and gave him some too. He twisted over onto his stomach and yelled out to Hank to get moving as he scooted and rolled away from the policemen's blows. Virgil made it as far as the edge of the court before he was forced to give up and ball into a knot to protect himself, and as he glanced out the corner of one blood-filled eye, Virgil realized with horror that Hank was still in the same spot, in the same position. In fact, Virgil realized with horror, from the moment his friend went down he had never moved again.

Hank Greenfield's skull had been crushed. Later, after his own injuries had been attended to, Virgil walked into ICU and saw his friend lying motionless in the bed. Hank was on life support and his family had gathered around him crying and praying.

"What in the world happened?" Hank's mother wanted to know, but Virgil didn't have an answer beyond what was obvious. They'd gotten jumped by some white kids and then almost killed by a bunch of redneck cops.

Hank died, and despite a local protest, the DA declined to press charges against the policemen who'd killed him. That was it for Virgil. He graduated from high school and headed straight out of the South. He had an aunt in New York City, and he bought a bus ticket and left Coffee, Mississippi, and was glad to be gone.

Virgil enrolled at John Jay College for four years and studied law enforcement. When he graduated with a degree in criminal justice, he immediately took the test for a corrections officer position and passed. By the time he was called for training at the academy he had been in the gym so often that he was rock hard and in top shape, and it was a good thing too. Working in a prison wasn't a job for punks, and the training program was intense. Virgil learned how to control the prisoners psychologically with a rigid system of rewards and punishments in order to avoid having to fight them every day. The most important things were a strong work ethic and mental toughness, and Virgil had plenty of both.

After he was hired Virgil was assigned a shift on Rikers Island where he met Frank Ramiro, a Dominican guy from Miami. Frank had come to New York a few years earlier on a division-two football scholarship. Frank found himself working at Rikers after getting booted out of school when he lost his scholarship due to too much partying. He got a girl pregnant after that, and her father stuck a gun in Frank's back and forced him to do the right thing. Before Frank knew it he had three kids in two years and a wife who had grand tastes.

Frank was one of the few correction officers who Virgil got tight with, and a couple of times a week they volunteered to pull double shifts to bring in extra money. But Ramiro started hanging out with a different group of other officers, and as time passed, Virgil noticed his friend wasn't down to pull doubles much anymore. Virgil was sharp as hell, and it only took him a minute to figure out the kind of mess his friend had gotten himself into.

"Hey, man," Virgil broke it down to Frank one night. "You know that scheme Olston and his boys got going?" Olston was a senior officer who was dirty as hell. Drugs flowed inside the jail just as hard as they flowed on the streets, and Virgil found out that Olston was running a game where officers were being used like carrier pigeons. He had his boys bringing the shit through the door unnoticed, then getting paid off by the capos and kingpins who distributed it on the inside.

Turning Olston down had been easy. Finding out that Frank had jumped on the dirty bandwagon was pretty damn hard. Virgil had been conflicted as hell, and what he knew gnawed at his gut night and day. He didn't believe in shortcuts. He had worked side by side with a man who scrubbed dirty toilets just to make ends meet, and anything less than honest work made Virgil uncomfortable and kept him from sleeping at night.

Frank was his boy, a real good officer, and Virgil mulled over the situation for weeks. He'd been put in a position where he basically had two choices: jump on the bandwagon and get down with the program, or mind his business and let Olston and his crew handle theirs. There was a third choice too, Virgil knew. One that bothered him on a lot of different levels but would ultimately satisfy the part of him that mattered most: his conscience.

"Dig this," he told Frank a few weeks later as they changed into civilian clothes after their shift. It had been real hard to work with his boy knowing what he knew, and over the past few weeks Virgil had put a lot of distance between them. He felt fucked up in the gut. Virgil had hung out with Frank's family. Ate at his mother's house and played with his kids. It was going to be even harder working without him, but if that's what it took for him to be able to close his eyes and sleep at night, then that's how it had to be. "You know me, Frank. You know how I think and how I get down. Certain things I can go for, and other things I just can't. I think you're a good officer, Frank. A good officer who's about to get caught up in some pretty bad shit."

Frank turned around slowly. "So what you trying to say, man?"

Virgil shrugged. "I ain't *trying* to say nothing. I'm saying it. I'm turning Olston and his crew in, Frank. I'm not trying to get you busted, and that's why I'm telling you first. You got a week to get yourself uninvolved in Olston's business, man. After that he goes down and anybody who gets caught with their hand in his pocket goes down too."

"Damn." Frank shook his head. "Do you know what you saying, man? You open your mouth on Olston and you'll be done on this rock. You'll never work another shift without looking over your shoulder. Every CO in a uniform is gonna come gunning for you, Virgil. Is that how you want it? You think you can survive around here after that?"

"Yeah," Virgil answered. He'd been raised to have faith in mankind. There were a whole lot more clean officers on the books than Frank knew. "Everybody ain't dirty, Frank. Some of us come to work to do an honest job, and we can't be bought by those penny-ante payoffs."

"Shit, Banks! I need this money, man. How you gonna do this to me?"

Virgil wasn't impressed. "Look at you, man. You

coming to work wearing a fucking Rolex. You don't *need* that kind of money, man. You just wanna get it without working for it. You're greedy, Frank, and what you're doing could get your little ass locked down for a good long stretch. Hell, you wanna be sitting in a cell with some of these same assholes we push around all day? I don't think so. Do yourself a favor, my friend. Get off Olston's roster unless you're ready to go down with him."

A week later Frank had pulled out of Olston's operation and Virgil turned ten of his fellow correctional officers in to internal affairs. There were a couple of rogue officers who tried to act up a little bit, but Virgil kept moving and let the bullshit roll off his shoulders. It was his morals that dictated his behavior, not his peers, and when it was all said and done, the only man Virgil had to be able to live with was Virgil.

To compensate him for his troubles, Virgil was rewarded with a pay raise and a transfer to Glattins Correctional Facility, a minimum-security prison in Westchester County. Trying to commute from Brooklyn to upper Westchester every day would have been as insane as it sounded, so Virgil packed his gear and moved into a small apartment about fifteen minutes away from the prison. The rent was cheap and the neighborhood was quiet, but the best thing about relocating to Glattins was that it gave Virgil a fresh start. The prison was expanding, and opportunities for advancement were there for those who wanted them. And Virgil did. He quickly became known as an officer who could be depended on. He worked hard, pulled extra shifts, and kept things professional with his fellow officers. He was in top shape and ran and worked out in his spare time. Let a knucklehead act up and Virgil was the kind of officer you wanted on your team. He had a talent for knowing the weak areas of the body, and whenever they got to scrapping with a prisoner Virgil would have the man screaming in submission with just a well-placed poke between two ribs or a quick thumb jab in the neck.

But something happened during his stint at Glattins that had come back to haunt Virgil. It was the sole reason that he was sitting in the death house wrestling with his soul while the death clock ticked down outside his window.

Virgil spent most weekends up at Glattins reading, working out, or watching movies, but occasionally he drove back down to Brooklyn and hung out with a few of his old friends. His boy Danny lived in Borough Park, and he had a sister who had caught Virgil's eye. He'd only talked to her twice, but the girl was bad and Virgil's nose was wide open, so when Danny invited him to a barbeque at his house and said his sister would be there, Virgil made sure he wasn't on the schedule for the weekend, then hauled ass down to Brooklyn right after his shift ended on Friday evening.

He was planning to crash at his boy Barrow's place, right down the street from Danny and his wife. Barrow was pulling a twenty-four-hour shift so Virgil would have the place all to himself, and he had just turned onto his street and parallel-parked along the curb when all hell broke loose.

Virgil was standing with one leg still inside the car when the sound of gunshots cracked through the air. He ducked and dove, banging his head against the top edge of the car, and spread himself across the front seats as flat as he could.

More shots rang out and he heard a woman scream in the distance. Virgil waited, expecting to hear more, and when he didn't he eased up and glanced outside. He had parked directly under a streetlight. The block was deserted. People had scattered in every direction, but Virgil knew plenty of folks were still around; peeking out of windows and from behind light poles, cars, and anything else they could find that might stop a stray bullet.

He heard nothing but silence, and after a few long

moments Virgil sat up and slowly opened his car door. His eyes scanned the shadows before he stepped outside, and he was still holding the door open when it happened.

A man came barreling across the street, sprinting toward him in dead run.

Virgil backed up and almost shut himself in the car door.

The guy was big. Dieseled. Barefoot and half-naked too. He had jet-black skin and muscles everywhere.

He was running at full speed, his bare feet papping hard and fast on the concrete. The man pumped his arms and sweat glistened on his bulging chest. Virgil stood frozen as their eyes met, and fear was in them both. They held gazes for less than three seconds, but for Virgil it was more than enough.

Blackwood! Virgil thought, *Who the fuck is he running from?*

Virgil winced as Isaiah cut in front of his car and passed directly under the streetlight. The man looked like a runaway slave. His whole back was roped up with thick scar tissue like a goddamn overseer had whipped the shit out of him with a cat-o'-nine-tails. Blackwood sped down the street and hopped a fence without breaking his stride. He disappeared from Virgil's line of sight and only then did Virgil move. He slammed his car door and scurried around the front end, then took off after Blackwood, moving as fast as he could.

But moments later Virgil's pursuit turned into an all-out scuffle as a team of cops pulled up behind him and jumped out running. Virgil was tackled from behind and ate a mouthful of concrete before he knew what the fuck was happening.

"Get down motherfucker!" a voice growled in his ear. An incredible weight came down on his back as his hands were jerked behind him so violently he damn near screamed.

"I'm with Corrections!" Virgil shouted, twisting to the side. "I'm a CO, man! I'm with Corrections!"

A foot pressed down hard on his head and Virgil could have sworn the son of a bitch was standing up on his face.

"I don't give a fuck who you with," the cop behind him said and slapped a pair of cuffs on him. "You hanging with the NYPD tonight."

The events of that night stayed on Virgil's mind for a long time.

And not because some fool had decided to take a

few shots at Reverend Al Sharpton while he was visiting a client in the neighborhood, and not just because Virgil had gotten his ass kicked and his nose broken by a few of New York's finest. No, that wasn't why, ten years after Isaiah Blackwood saved him from a throat cutting, Virgil repaid the solid by getting stomped into the ground while Blackwood ran into the night and got away with attempted murder.

"I told y'all motherfuckers I was with Corrections!" Virgil said after they had dragged his ass down to the precinct and checked him out.

"Then why the fuck was you running like that?"

This was the same fool who had stood on his goddamn head, and Virgil wanted to smash his ass.

Instead he stared at him for a long moment. There'd always been an undercurrent of tension between police and corrections officers, with police usually coming out on top. Cops had very little respect for the job corrections officers did every day, and there was no love lost between the two groups regardless if they were black or white.

But these motherfuckers here hadn't even given him the minimum courtesy that was usually granted between all men involved in law enforcement. They'd treated him like a no-count nigger, like some black piece of shit who had committed the crime of breathing in some of their air.

"I was chasing the guy you were looking for," he said finally. "He ran right toward me, then crossed the street in front of my car."

"Oh, you must be one of those convict sitters who wants to carry a gun. You must've forgot—that's our fuckin job, not yours. Next time call a real cop."

"Fine." Virgil nodded. He reached across the table and retrieved his watch, wallet, and a ring that they'd taken from him when they brought him in.

"But since you saw the guy, tell us what he looked like."

Virgil walked over to the door and stopped. Isaiah Blackwood had once saved his life. These fools behind him wouldn't have hesitated to take it. He looked over his shoulder at the rednecked fucker who had jerked his hand behind his back and almost folded his arm up like a chicken wing and chuckled.

"I can't remember. I guess I forgot."

But the next day he was remembering all over again.

"Old Reverend Al almost got tagged last night."

Virgil nodded at his friend. He was sitting in Danny's

backyard with Danny and his sister Melinda, who worked as a records supervisor in the county clerk's office. Virgil's right shoulder still throbbed and the side of his face was scuffed. It was his pride that hurt him the most, though, and it was pride that stopped him from going back to that police station and telling those boys exactly who he'd seen last night. He fumed inside. Why the hell Blackwood had been out taking shots at Al Sharpton was anybody's guess, but that type of stupidity was beyond criminal. It was almost insane.

"I heard Sharpton was on his way to see the family of that old woman," Danny continued. "The one the cops shot and killed when they kicked down the wrong door."

"But did you hear what happened to that white lady and her daughter last night?" Melinda asked.

Virgil was trying to eat a chicken wing without getting the sticky sweet barbeque sauce all over his fingers. He sat up and accepted the napkin she offered him and wiped his hands. Melinda was a real lady. Soft, smart, well-spoken. He wanted to know her better.

"No. What happened to them?" He had been too embarrassed to tell his friends that he'd gotten his ass kicked the night before. He'd skulked into Barrow's house and licked his wounds in private.

Melinda frowned. "They were almost killed. She's

my neighbor from down the hall, and she told me a guy climbed up her fire escape and broke into her house through her daughter's bedroom window. My neighbor heard her daughter crying and ran into her room and found a man in there. He forced my friend to strip out of all her clothes, and he had just taken off his clothes too when somebody started shooting outside.

"She started screaming, and I guess that scared him off because he ran out onto the fire escape and got away."

Virgil saw the terror in Melinda's eyes and it touched him.

"My friend was frightened senseless and so was her little daughter." Melinda sighed and took a sip of her Sprite. "And it used to be so nice around here. I just don't know what this neighborhood is coming to."

Virgil leaned toward her. He wished he could kiss the worry lines off of her face. "Did your friend find out who the guy was? I mean, were the cops able to catch him?"

Melinda shook her head. "No. I don't think they did. She went to stay at her mother's house for a while. Her husband is a fireman. He was on shift last night, and of course he's fit to be tied."

"Well, did she get a good look at him? Did she tell you what he looked like?"

Melinda shrugged. "He was black, she knew that much. A pretty big guy too, from what she said."

Virgil watched the worry lines deepen on her face and a knot of fear formed in his stomach.

"It all happened so fast that that's about all she could remember. Except for his back. She said he ran out of there wearing nothing but his underwear, and he had some kind of hideous burn all over his back."

The circus was in full swing outside, and next door the command post was buzzing with last-minute preparations. Virgil leaned back in his chair and closed his eyes, his mind darting to and fro, searching for an avenue he might have somehow missed before.

It had been five short years since he'd married Melinda Allen. Five short years since some nut had taken a crack shot at Al Sharpton on a hot summer night in Borough Park, and five short years since the young white woman, whom he now knew as Melinda's friend and neighbor, Felicia Tate, had been accosted in her own apartment.

Virgil had been crushed when he heard about the murders of Terrie Mills and her daughter, and when he found out who they'd arrested an enormous wave of guilt had swept over him, sickening him in his soul. For the first time in over ten years he'd called in sick to work and stayed in bed for three whole days.

Fuck the debt he'd owed Isaiah Blackwood.

Virgil had underestimated that bastard. Blackwood was more than just a career criminal, he was a cancer on society. If Virgil had to do it all over again he would rather have had that Mexican kid slit his throat instead of letting Blackwood get away that summer night just to slit Terrie Mills's throat a few years later. No matter how pissed off he'd been with those cracker cops, Virgil should have turned Blackwood's ass in, and he knew his decision to let him slide would probably haunt him for the rest of his life.

But some months later, after the trial and Blackwood's conviction and sentencing, Virgil got to witness some what goes around coming back around when he found out Blackwood was being sent upstate to the prison he'd been made warden of in Quincy. He'd almost yelled out loud when that fool decided to drop his legal appeals and let the necessary occur, and Virgil had been happy to lock Blackwood's black ass down in the deepest recesses of death row.

Like most New Yorkers and concerned citizens throughout the country, Virgil was fed up with the endless number of career criminals who terrorized the nation and kept good, working people too scared to venture off their porches at night. About a year ago, right after Melinda discovered they were going to have their second child, Virgil's wife had been knocked down to the ground on a busy street in Manhattan and her purse was snatched off her arm.

It was God's grace that neither she nor the baby had been hurt, but if Virgil could have gotten his hands on the lowlife thief who had put his damn hands on his wife, he would have killed him. No doubt about it. He would have killed him dead.

And that's why he could understand the rage of blood-lust that was running through America's veins tonight. It wasn't just Terrie and Arielle Mills who Blackwood had to pay for, but so many other victims of random crime in New York City who were simply mad as hell and not taking it anymore.

Three days ago Virgil had felt the same way. True, he would have preferred it if the execution had been scheduled for somebody else's prison, but it seemed as if his life was inexplicably linked with Blackwood's, and no matter what he did or where he went, Blackwood always managed to show up.

With Blackwood's criminal history and the guilt trip

Virgil had been on for the four years since Terrie Mills and her daughter had been murdered, there was no doubt about it, Virgil would have flipped the switch on Blackwood all by himself if he could have. But something had happened two days ago that set Virgil's whole world on end. He'd been rocked off his feet by a realization so bone-chilling and heart-stopping that for the past forty-eight hours he'd been running around on desperate mode, searching for help and panicking like hell.

It had happened when they were taking Blackwood for his pre-execution physical. State law mandated that all condemned prisoners be examined by a physician, and Virgil had been standing outside Blackwood's cell while the guards performed a mandatory body cavity check before they moved him.

Virgil watched them handle the prisoner, contempt heavy in his eyes. There were all kinds of criminals be-hind these walls, but prison held its own court for men like Isaiah Blackwood, pedophiles who got off on hurting women and little kids. He'd been coded a "short eyes" by the other inmates. A child rapist. He spent twenty-three hours of each day in his cell, and he was heavily guarded during exercise and shower breaks. Virgil had ordered Blackwood be put on a strict suicide watch ever since he dropped his appeals. There was no way in hell he was going to let his prisoner cheat the good people of New York out of his death.

Virgil noticed how the guards spoke to Blackwood in quiet tones, the kind reserved for the few inmates they respected. It was true that Blackwood hadn't given them any problems at all over the years. He was strong but quiet and agreeable. He never raised his voice or complained, and he let the COs do their jobs without impeding them in any way.

"All right, Blackwood. Time to go. Remove your clothing, man. Thanks. Now open your mouth. Stick out your feet. Cool. Now hold them up. Turn around. Bend over. All right. Stand up straight. Turn back around for me—"

"Wait!" Virgil had pushed into the cell and slung a guard out of his way. Blackwood stood there naked, staring down at Virgil from a blank, expressionless face. "Turn back around," Virgil ordered. Blackwood's bicep was like a rock as Virgil grabbed his arm and peered around him.

Blackwood obeyed without saying a word, and as Virgil stood there staring at the smooth, unmarred skin on the man's jet-black muscular back, a sinking feeling swept over him as he realized that he'd been dead wrong. Perhaps they'd all been wrong. Maybe they'd been so fucking wrong that in about forty-eight hours the state of New York might just open up that death chamber, strap Isaiah Blackwood to an electrified chair, and execute an innocent man.

Virgil was a man on a mission.

He had two days to find the truth and maybe save them all from making an unforgivable mistake, and the first person he called was Melinda.

"Hon, you remember the night Al Sharpton got shot at and that guy broke into your friend Felicia Tate's window, don't you?"

Melinda remembered just perfectly. Virgil told her what she needed and minutes later he was banging away on his computer keyboard, deep in Isaiah Blackwood's electronic file. He retrieved all the information he could get from the Department of Corrections, then started scouring the internet where details of the crime were available in abundance. Within thirty minutes he got an email from Melinda, complete with a file attachment.

Virgil waited as the large document downloaded, and when it was done he saved the contents to a special file he'd created on his desktop. His baby had come through for him. She'd sent PDF copies of transcripts, witness statements, and everything else he needed to gain a better picture of Isaiah Blackwood and his sham of a trial.

After examining a couple of sworn statements and then cross-referencing them with a witness list, Virgil made another call.

"This is Virgil Banks calling from the Department of Corrections. I'm looking for Deborah James. Is she available?"

Minutes later he had Isaiah Blackwood's girlfriend on the line. According to the documents Virgil had read, she'd testified for the defense, although the transcript showed the prosecution had basically chomped on her ass and turned everything she said around to suit their own purposes.

"I have a quick question for you," Virgil said. He could tell she was suspicious by the way she hesitated, stalling in her response.

"Umm, well I already told my story a long time ago and I don't really know nothing else . . ."

"That's okay," Virgil said, making his voice go deep with authority. "My question is quick and simple, and if there's anybody in this world who knows the answer to it, I'm confident that it's you."

Deborah was silent, waiting for the shoe to drop as Virgil delved right in.

"Does Isaiah Blackwood have any kind of disfiguring marks on his body? Any scars? More specifically, does Isaiah have a large burn on his back?"

"Nah," Deborah answered quickly, sounding relieved that the question was too simple to trip her up. "Shyne doesn't have any kind of marks like that." She hesitated half a second and then added, "But Shug does."

Virgil placed an emergency call to Janet Lovitz, the DA who had prosecuted the murder case almost four years earlier. "Ms. Lovitz, so glad I caught you. I've got some information about the Isaiah Blackwood case that is guaranteed to blow your mind."

Janet came across a bit cool on the phone, but after Virgil pressed her and shared a few of his suspicions, she agreed to meet him for lunch the next day. Virgil was up studying Blackwood's case file the whole night, and the next morning just before dawn, he drove down to the city and was sitting at a small table in the Coffee Grind when she arrived.

Janet was a plain but not totally unattractive white woman who Virgil estimated could have been anywhere from thirty-five to fifty. She wore a no-nonsense look and had a reputation for being a real ball-buster in the courtroom. Virgil had read the transcripts, and without a doubt she had busted Isaiah Blackwood's balls during his trial.

She listened quietly and sipped iced tea while Virgil laid his theory out on the table.

"Do you remember an incident where Al Sharpton was shot at in Borough Park?" As exhausted as Virgil was, his voice was high-pitched and trembling with excitement.

Janet thought for a brief moment, then nodded.

"Well, that was the same night that another white woman, Felicia Tate, and her young daughter were attacked in a building right next door. I believe that whoever broke into Mrs. Tate's window that night is the same person who killed Terrie Mills and her daughter. And it couldn't have been Isaiah Blackwood."

Whatever reaction Virgil had been hoping to see in Janet's eyes never materialized. The look she gave him was as cold as her tea.

"And that's the grand theory you came all the way to Brooklyn to lay on me?"

Virgil nodded. "But it's more than just a theory, Ms. Lovitz. The way I see it, the pieces of this puzzle fit perfectly. Isaiah Blackwood might be innocent, and no matter what dumb-ass decisions he's made about his appeals, we've gotta stop that execution tomorrow night."

Janet shook her head once, a practiced, dismissive move.

"Sorry. The law doesn't consider theories and speculation when criminal punishment is being doled out. We deal with hard evidence, and what you're saying is so far-fetched that in the end it doesn't really matter. Isaiah Blackwood was convicted in a court of law and sentenced to death by a judge who had complete authority and jurisdiction over his case. That's not going to change because you believe you've found a new piece to an old puzzle."

"But everything I just told you casts doubt on the case," Virgil insisted. "Even if you don't believe me, the least you have to do in good conscience is take another look at things and see where these new facts lead you."

"The facts already led us to Terrie and Arielle Mills's killer. Isaiah is no Boy Scout, Mr. Banks. I'm sure you've seen his rap sheet. It's so long you could wrap it around your head and wear it as a turban."

"I'm not disputing that. He's a career criminal, that's obvious. But he didn't commit this particular crime. I'm almost sure of it."

Janet Lovitz shook her head and pushed her glass away.

"Look, Mr. Banks. Isaiah's DNA was found under

Terrie Mills's fingernails, and two hairs from her daughter were matched to him as well. That kind of evidence can't be discounted."

"But the MO in the Mills murder is exactly the same as in that case in Borough Park! My wife knows Felicia Tate and she actually saw the perp as he was running away from the scene! The woman said he ran out of there in nothing except a pair of drawers, and I saw him that night too. I looked dead in his eyes, Ms. Lovitz, and twenty-four hours ago I would have put my right hand on my mother's grave and sworn that the guy who ran past me that night was Isaiah Blackwood! But it wasn't. I did some checking. Isaiah was in state custody at the time, and the guy I saw had a thick scar all over his back. It was ugly as hell. Like a really bad keloid, and Felicia Tate and her daughter saw it too."

Virgil lowered his voice and shifted his chair closer to the table. "I made a couple of calls last night, and I don't know how else to say this but Isaiah Blackwood has never had a scar on his back. But his brother, Gabriel, our candidate for mayor, certainly does."

Janet's reaction came strictly from a position of white power.

"You people always amaze me. I thought you said you'd done your homework? I'm well aware of the fact that Gabriel Blackwood has a disfiguring scar on his back, Mr. Banks. It's a burn, actually, and I'm the one who put it there. If you had looked a little further then you would know that Isaiah and Gabriel Blackwood are twins. Identical twins. As such, they share identical DNA."

Virgil's mouth dropped wide open.

She continued, "You were right that there was no DNA found at the scene of the Tate break-in." Janet tilted her head slightly and peered at him. "But I did a little homework myself, Mr. Banks. Weren't *you* arrested and questioned that night? Yes, Isaiah was incarcerated, but Gabriel had an alibi. It was dark in the room and Mrs. Tate never saw his face. When she rushed to the window, she barely saw him from behind. You're the only one who claims to have clearly seen one of the Blackwood brothers that night, yet your sworn statement to the police indicated that you couldn't identify the guy you were chasing. How would you explain that?"

Virgil's heart went cold.

"Where was Gabriel Blackwood the night of the Mills murders?" he asked in a whisper.

"At his mother's house. Comforting her after Isaiah's drunken outburst. She testified that he never left her house once that night."

"She's lying."

"You can't prove that."

"But Gabriel testified at the trial that his brother and Terrie Mills had fought earlier in the day, right? The victim went crazy and started a fight. That could explain how Isaiah's DNA got under her fingernails."

Janet nodded. "True, but how do you explain the pubic hair that was found in Arielle's underwear? That was his too."

"They're twins. Their DNA is identical, remember? Who's to say it was Isaiah's? Maybe it was Gabriel's."

Janet's voice was cool. "Maybe it was. Maybe it wasn't. But who cares? One of them is no better than the other."

Virgil stared at Janet in disbelief. "What the hell are you? Some kind of fuckin' headhunter? Don't you give a damn which Blackwood brother you hang? I guess as long as there's a black neck swinging from your legal noose that's all that counts!"

"I'm not a racist," Janet said calmly. "I'm a realist. A realist and a warrior for battered women everywhere. Face it, Banks. There's no way in hell we could've gotten to Gabriel Blackwood. We were under a lot of public pressure for an arrest, and we got one."

"Fuck pressure!" Virgil exploded. "You can live with

pressure! Can you live with an innocent man's blood on your hands while a murderer walks the streets?"

"Look," Janet said calmly. "Gabriel 'Rashawn' Black-wood might very well be guilty as sin, but his alibi was tight and his credibility was way too high. But you seem like a smart man. Haven't you ever heard the expression, 'There's more than one way to skin a cat'? Gabriel may have been beyond my reach but Isaiah was easy. And accessible. Let Gabriel and his conscience wrestle with his brother's death. If Isaiah is really innocent, then wouldn't Gabriel step up and confess? The bottom line is, I did my job and the jury found Isaiah Blackwood guilty. And now the chips are falling down around his brother's shoulders, and that's exactly where they be-long."

The ride back to Quincy was a bitch.

Virgil was so exhausted he wanted to hold his eyes open with one hand and drive with the other. To say he was disappointed in Janet Lovitz wouldn't come close to what he really wanted to say. Lovitz was a dirty DA, and she'd practically admitted it. If she was really responsible for the burn on Gabriel Blackwood's back, then that meant the two of them were tight enough to be in each other's personal space, and that alone should have been enough to disqualify her from the case.

Fuck it, Virgil muttered. He made it back to Quincy and went straight to his office and put in a call to the governor.

"I'm sorry, Warden Banks. Governor Spitzer is unavailable at this time. I'll give him your message and ask him to return your call."

Virgil typed an urgent request asking the governor to contact him immediately, then faxed it from his office. He called Melinda next and had a thirty-minute conversation with her. She respected his integrity and had his back. She promised to rally every single resource she could find and set a team of internet investigators on Gabriel Blackwood's ass right away. But what about right now?

Desperation crawled around in Virgil's belly and swelled in his throat. Isaiah Blackwood was going to die tonight, and his foul, politicking brother was going to stand there and watch the whole thing go down.

Janet Lovitz had been right about one thing. He was riding on little more than some circumstantial speculation and a gritty feeling in his gut. No, he couldn't prove the wrong Blackwood brother was sitting downstairs in his holding cell waiting to die, but he couldn't live with the possibility of it either.

It took him five minutes to get downstairs to the small holding cell where condemned prisoners were to receive their last visitors. The room was clean and well lit, and ironically painted in soothing tones.

Isaiah Blackwood looked up as Virgil entered. His head had been shaved earlier in the day, and they'd allowed him to take a shower and change into a clean white jumpsuit.

The two men looked at each other with probing, questioning eyes. Virgil was struck by Blackwood's size and physique, an athlete's body with a criminal's soul. He searched the prisoner's eyes and was surprised by what he didn't find. Fear. Resistance. Not even a trace. Instead, Blackwood was noble. Fearless. Standing firm and defiant in the face of death. Virgil stepped closer to him. Some fools needed saving from themselves.

Neither spoke for long minutes, then Virgil broke the silence.

"Why are you here?"

It took Blackwood a long time to respond, and when he did he offered little more than a shrug.

"What kind of question is that?"

"I don't think you belong here."

Blackwood laughed, the whiteness of his teeth cutting a path across his dark face. He nodded toward the door where guards from the execution team were posted. "Well I wish you'd go tell them two motherfuckers out there that."

Virgil lowered himself into a chair. "Why didn't you tell the whole world when you had a chance?"

Blackwood shook his head slowly, gazing at Virgil from hooded eyes. "Man, what do you want? If there's a point to all this just go ahead and get to it. I ain't got a whole lot of time, in case you haven't noticed. Why you wasting it?"

"Because I don't think you belong here. At least not for this crime. What really went down with Terrie Mills and her daughter that night?"

Blackwood sat up straight and stared across the table. "I already told all I'm gonna tell. To you and everybody else. I got convicted, remember? Don't you trust the justice system? You a part of it. Why you doubting it now?"

"Because I know you didn't do it. I read your testimony, man. You were drunk, and you were loud. You talked a lot of shit, and you pissed off a lot of folks, your mother included. But you didn't kill Terrie, Isaiah. Sure, you might have smacked her up and y'all tussled just like your brother said in court. But the reason you can't remember killing Terrie or raping her daughter is because you didn't do it."

Virgil paused.

"But I bet you know who did."

Blackwood frowned and shook his head. "You talking shit, man. I—"

They fell silent as the sound of footsteps fell in the hall. One of the guards slid the cell door open by its bars, and when Virgil saw who stood waiting on the tier, he faced Isaiah quickly and pleaded with his prisoner in a hushed, desperate voice.

"Go ahead and put a stop to this, Blackwood. You can call this shit off at any time, and I'll send everybody packing the hell up out of here. You've got a legal right to do it. So get behind your appeals, man, and give me a chance to help you. I'll talk to the governor, the DA— anybody I have to—just get your lawyer to reinstate your appeals, and I'll do every damn thing in my power to see to it that the right guy is sitting here while the innocent man walks free."

"No." Blackwood shook his head firmly. "No."

Bitterness and frustration surged inside Virgil as Blackwood's visitors stood in the doorway, waiting to enter. Virgil stood up from the chair and exhaustion almost buckled his knees. Tears of frustration welled in his bloodshot eyes as he cried out to his condemned prisoner in disbelief, "Man, why the *hell* are you doing this to yourself? Give me one good reason why you won't put a stop to this shit!"

Blackwood just smiled. "I can give you two," he said calmly, then looked beyond Virgil and nodded first at his brother and then at his mother. "Loyalty and love."

In the darkness of an office adjacent to the command post, Virgil was sitting with his head down on the desk when an officer knocked, then opened the door.

"Sir. It's eleven-twenty. They need you in the death chamber by eleven-thirty."

He squinted into the crack of light that spilled into the room, then sat up straight in the chair and nodded.

"Right. I'll be there. Thank you."

Virgil took a deep breath and begged his savior. *Lord, please have mercy on us all for what we are about to do. Please have mercy on Blackwood for what he's already done.* He walked over to the window and looked out once more. Oddly, the crowd had calmed down quite a bit. The time was drawing near. The protesters were all ears as the town crier announced over his microphone, "Forty minutes until the execution."

Virgil lit another cigarette and took three hard puffs. Melinda and a few of her close friends in the police department had been working just as hard as he had. They'd compiled a list for him and began following a paper trail that Virgil was absolutely sure would end at the feet of a killer. Even though it would be too late. He crushed his cigarette in the ashtray. It was time to go. Virgil walked out of the command post filled with dread, and accompanied by two highly trained guards, he buttoned his jacket and strode down the hall toward the death chamber.

It took a specially trained crew of officers to conduct an execution, and Virgil's handpicked team was composed of some of the best and brightest officers the prison had to offer. They'd undergone two weeks of training sessions, eight hours each day, and were more than ready to perform their duties. Two dress rehearsals had already been conducted, one the day before and the other just a few hours ago. Pre-execution checks were being performed when Virgil entered the death chamber, and he headed straight for the team leader to receive his report.

"Sir," the large, burly young man snapped straight as an arrow as Virgil approached. Roland Martin was a damned good officer, but Virgil had been thinking about much more than his job credentials a few weeks ago when he selected him to head the execution team. Martin stood about six four and weighed an easy three hundred pounds. Even though he worked out and ran, there was still something pudgy about him but Virgil didn't care. He'd chosen Martin because he was just as big as Blackwood and he had a little cushioning on him too. If Blackwood decided to get rough Virgil was sure this corn-fed white boy could match him head up until the rest of the team could get him under control.

"The medical doctor is standing by, the chaplain is on deck, and all the legal documents are signed and in order. We're ready."

Virgil glanced around the room and nodded at his team of volunteers. None of them had ever witnessed an execution before but all of them had enough smarts to read the state directives and carry them out. How much sense did it take to kill a man anyway?

As the warden, Virgil was required to play a key role in the execution, and knowing what he knew about Isaiah Blackwood was going to test him in the core. He had his doubts about the looney-ass prison doctor too and whether the man could actually go through with it. The state required the staff doctor to be on hand and physically witness the execution, but earlier in the day he'd come to Virgil and mumbled something about how he would rather wait outside the chamber until the prisoner was dead before coming in.

Virgil didn't give a damn about what the doctor wanted, and he didn't pull any punches when he told him that either. Every man on the crew had a job to do, regardless of how hard it might be. Somebody had to watch the heart monitor and the brain-wave machine, and Virgil planned to hold the doctor's big feet to the fire and make the man do his damn job. Hell, the law said Virgil had to be in the death chamber too, to monitor the inmate in case he showed any signs of pain or suffering during the procedure. And if any signs of suffering were detected, then Virgil was supposed to halt the execution immediately and allow the doctor to revive the man. Just so they could get him in good enough shape to kill him all over again.

Virgil took a deep breath and swiped his hand down his face, an unforgivable sense of failure swelling in his heart. He'd walked through life guided by his conscience and trying to do what was right, but it had suddenly become obvious that he was just another black man caught in the prison system. Even from the other side of the bars. But he couldn't do for Isaiah Blackwood what the man refused to do for himself. Virgil couldn't make him switch places with his own brother to save his own life. He could jump up and down and curse out the DA, defy the governor and refuse to take part in the execution. He could even turn his back and walk out the door, throw away his life's work and camp out on the steps of the Supreme Court, and it still wouldn't matter. For men like Isaiah Blackwood, liberty was nothing more than a state of mind. Virgil had spent his professional career trusting that justice would be exacted in the courts but this time, he feared, justice would have to be meted out by the Lord.

OCTOBER 2007

THE OBSERVATION ROOM

Janet Lovitz entered the observation room followed closely by Leslie Hemp, the state-appointed victim's services coordinator. The lights were dim and the bolted chairs had been designed theater-style, with a metal railing partitioning the seating area from an area covered in dark drapes.

"We've assigned you five seats over there." Janet pointed toward the far side of the room. Witnesses for the victim's family were always brought into the death chamber first and escorted out last. Three guards were posted in their area as a precaution.

Several weeks earlier Janet had received the names of the five people whom Terrie's mother, Anna, wanted to be present for the execution of her daughter's murderer. Janet had been shocked and irritated to find Della Blackwood's name included on that list as a witness for the crime victim. It had amazed Janet to watch Gabriel and Isaiah's mother during the trial, sitting on the prosecution's side of the courtroom and crying just as loudly as the Mills family.

Sure, Mrs. Blackwood's obvious entrenchment on the side of the victim had sent a strong message to the jury and played a vital role in helping Janet swing the case, but still. A mother's first sympathies should be with her child, regardless of what he'd done. Janet thought of her own mother and the steadfast loyalty she espoused, and it made her wonder what kind of life the Blackwood brothers might have had to make them both turn out the way they did.

In the privacy of her office Janet had compared the prosecution list to the one submitted by the defense council, and when she saw the woman listed twice she had quietly scratched Mrs. Blackwood's name off her list and allowed her to remain on the one submitted by her son.

A prison officer beckoned, and Janet watched as the

victim's services coordinator guided Paula Mills, Terrie's sisters, and Arielle's father, Ben, into the observation room. It had been close to four years since their loss, but the pain they continued to suffer was evident on their faces.

"It's almost over," Janet bent down and whispered to Paula Mills, grasping the woman's cold hands between her own. "Soon Terrie and Arielle will be able to rest in peace, and you and your family will be able to live in peace as well."

A group of seven reporters quietly entered the room. They looked around nervously, then shuffled over to the seats that had been designated for them. It was a mixed team of males and females who represented the Associated Press and United Press International, and other selected representatives from various print and broadcast media outlets, and each of them felt lucky to have been chosen to witness this monumental event.

Deborah James filed into the observation room alone. Her hands were clasped in front of her and she looked terrified. Soft murmurs filled the air as the witnesses whispered among themselves, but Deborah ignored the voices and kept her gaze downcast. She'd been crying and her hands were cold. Unable to resist, she took a quick peak at the curtain-covered area to her front, and her knees wobbled as she realized what was on the other side of the heavy black cloth.

A ball of fear clogged her throat and she struggled for her next breath. She was so damned scared. Scared for Shyne. Scared of what kind of pain he was about to face.

But Shyne wasn't scared for himself. She had arrived at Quincy in time to get a few minutes alone with him and she'd wept nonstop as he did his best to comfort her in his last hours.

"Baby, I'm sorry this is happening," she'd whispered between tears as Shyne gazed at her with a calm look in his eyes. "I'm sorry for everything bad that's ever happened." Deborah had cried so hard she had to wipe her nose on the sleeve of her shirt, and she'd cried even harder when Shyne told her that he'd never loved her more than he did at that moment.

"You just take care of yourself and Samitra," he had insisted. "Don't worry about me. I made my own choices, baby, and I'm ready for this." He'd grinned at her then, and although Deborah knew her man could be very bad, all the good things about him were there in his smile.

"Watch out for my mama when you go out there," he joked. "Okay? She's liable to mess around and start a fight if you ain't careful."

Despite her sadness, Deborah had grinned a little bit

too. "I ain't thinking about your crazy-ass mama, Shyne. But I'm never gonna stop thinking about you."

Deborah sat in the observation room and replayed that last conversation in her mind, drawing strength from it. As bad as she was hurting, she felt proud of Shyne tonight. The whole world was falling down around him, but he was a calm spot in the middle of a raging storm. He wasn't even the same man that he'd been when he was out on the streets. Something about him had changed while he was in prison. Deborah had noticed it right after the trial when he dropped his appeals and refused to fight his death sentence.

"Are you crazy?" she'd screamed when he called and told her he was giving up all appeals. "You do that and they're gonna kill your ass, Shyne! Gilbert is a damn good lawyer, you know that, baby. You went through that whole trial and everything! When they find out you didn't do this shit we'll sue the state of New York for so much money, all them fuckers is gonna drop, roll, and go bankrupt!"

Shyne had been quiet on the other end of the phone, and no matter how loud she screamed, Deborah could tell he was out of her reach.

"Don't worry about me, baby," he'd told her before hanging up, and little did she know that that phrase would become his battle cry. "I've spent my whole life doing crazy shit for money. Right now I'm working strictly for love."

And right now Deborah was able to feel that love just by listening to Shyne's voice echo in her ear. She held on to it and let it wrap her in comfort, and when she looked up and saw Shug and Della walking in, she swallowed her tears and nodded as they took their seats beside her.

"You okay?" Shug asked. Deborah nodded as he hugged her briefly before turning to seat his mother. "Mama? How about you?"

Della nodded, and Shug put his arm around her shoulders and glanced around the room. A team of reporters were present, and he nodded at a few he recognized. He knew there wouldn't be any cameras or audio recorders allowed in the witness chamber, but he noted that several reporters were writing on small white pads, so he clutched Della to him and pressed his cheek to her hair.

"Paula's over there," Della said, breaking free and looking across the room. "I thought I was supposed to be sitting with her and Ben?"

Shug smirked. The whole time they were in the death cell with Shyne, Della hadn't spoken a word. It had been awkward for all of them, and despite his attempts to draw her out, Della had allowed her last opportunity to talk to her youngest son slip by.

"You thought wrong, Mama. That's the victim's section over there. How would it look if you were sitting with those people at a time like this? Those reporters over there may not have cameras, but they do have pens. We're here for Shyne, remember?"

"I'm here because you made me—"

"Mr. Blackwood."

Gabriel turned and looked at the man who had slipped into the seat beside him.

He nodded. "Warden Banks."

Gabriel held out his hand. Virgil glanced down but didn't take it.

"How's the campaign going?"

Gabriel allowed himself a pained smile. "Good. Very good considering the circumstances."

"Yeah," Virgil grunted. "So, when's the last time you've been out hunting—I mean campaigning—in Borough Park?"

Gabriel looked surprised. "Excuse me, man? I didn't get that."

"You remember Felicia Tate and her daughter, right?"

"Sorry." Gabriel shrugged. "That name doesn't ring a bell."

"Yeah," Virgil said again. Then softly. "I bet it hurt like hell, huh? You know, when you got that burn on your back?"

"What?"

Virgil laughed. "Come on, now. No need to front. But tell me. Did she look any better back in the day? Janet Lovitz? I always heard that if you had to fool around with a white girl you should at least pick one who looked like something. I just can't figure out why she's so damn mad at you, man. Mad enough to get back at you in any way she can. What'd you do to piss her off? Make her put a paper bag over her head?"

Gabriel glanced around. Across the middle aisle several guards stood quietly with their hands at their sides. On the left he saw Terrie's family, sitting calmly and staring straight ahead. He shifted around in his seat until his back was to Della and he was facing the warden.

"You're way out of line, Mr. Banks," Gabriel said in his most professional voice. "I'm here with my family at a very vulnerable and personal time. I'd appreciate it if you'd respect that."

"Respect, shit." Virgil chuckled. "Just tell it like it is, man. You're here to make sure nobody ever finds out the truth. But they will, I guarantee it. Because if anybody should be frying in that chair tonight, it's you. And

I swear on my mother I'm gonna make sure the world knows it."

"You accusing me of something?" Gabriel growled, coming out of his ghetto bag. "Mess with me, you dumb fuck, and I'll have my lawyers all over your uneducated black ass in a hot minute. Believe it."

Virgil chuckled and stood up, buttoning his jacket.

"You don't scare me with that street talk, man. You just piss me off."

Gabriel shook his head. "Nigger, they might have tossed you a badge and dressed you up in a suit, but you're just as worthless as these fucking prisoners you got locked up in here."

"Perhaps." Virgil nodded. "But the whole world is gonna know what you did, Blackwood. You can kiss Gracie Mansion good-bye, my brother. The only way you're getting inside that crib is if you climb up the fire escape and break in through the window, because I'm gonna make sure everybody knows exactly who you are and exactly what you did."

"Man, what the hell are you talking about?" Gabriel demanded.

"He's your brother, man. Your own fucking brother."

The look that crossed Gabriel's face was priceless. It was only there for a flash, for a hint of a second, but it was there and Virgil recognized it for what it was. Guilt.

Gabriel shrugged. "I still don't know what you're talking about. And why the hell are you sweating me, man? I tell you what. You getting burnt out behind these walls? You need a little change of pace?" Gabriel slipped his hand into his jacket pocket. "Well I've got a job waiting for you when I get elected." He tossed his business card in the air. "Call me."

Virgil caught the card and crushed it in his fist. "Oh, you'll get a call, all right. I can promise you that. And it's going to come in loud and clear. Time is up, motherfucker. Not just for your brother, but for you too."

TICKTOCK
12 O'CLOCK

SHYNE It was just after midnight when they came for me.

Four of them. Trained up and ready for a fight.

I was sitting on the edge of the cot when the lock clicked and the door slid back on its track. I knew these guys and they had nothing to fear from me. Still, they rolled into my cell like a band of riot police.

I stood up slowly and waited. Everybody in the cell was breathing hard except me.

"Blackwood, Isaiah Raynard."

I nodded.

"It's time to go, man."

It was Roberts who had spoken, a CO who had a reputation for brutality.

I held out my hands without making a sound. There was a female officer near the door and she looked nervous, like she was expecting the worst. But Roberts extended the cuffs with cool respect in his eyes, and I stayed easy and allowed him to clamp them on me. First my wrists, and then my ankles.

We left the cell and walked down a short hall that led to the death chamber. I didn't drag my feet, but I didn't rush either. I was a pretty big guy with wide shoulders and good-sized arms. Even with the irons and the cuffs I could've wrecked some shit if I wanted to, but I didn't. I made it my business to walk down that hall the same way I had walked into this joint. Like a man.

OCTOBER 12, 2007

THE DEATH CHAMBER

Virgil watched as the condemned man entered the death chamber flanked by four guards. Blackwood looked around the room as his cuffs and irons were removed, his eyes resting lightly on each person before settling on the chair.

It sat close to the far wall and Virgil thought the sight of it was enough to make a man act a fool, but nothing about Blackwood changed when he saw it. Blackwood had chosen the chair as the instrument of his death, but he could have easily been looking at a houseplant or a dirt bike. He gave it no more energy than one would give a candle or a telephone, and Virgil felt a tremendous surge of respect for the criminal who stood before him cooler than a cucumber and completely unfazed in the presence of his own death.

Blackwood looked at Virgil with an unshakable conviction in his eyes, and Virgil couldn't help but be bitter as he thought about those original two brothers who found themselves out of favor with God. Cain had killed Abel. Gabriel wasn't killing Isaiah, but he wasn't saving him either.

Virgil nodded toward the team chief, and when directed, Blackwood stepped boldly over to the chair. He sat down and stared straight ahead as he was strapped in by two guards from the restraint team. The curtains between the chamber and the observation room were raised, and something enormous swelled in Virgil as he met Gabriel's gaze in the crowd. It was a ball of helpless outrage, and he fought it down as a tape recorder was turned on and a microphone and a printed citation were pushed into his hands to be read.

"This is a recording of the execution of Isaiah Raynard Blackwood on October 12th, 2007. My name is Virgil Banks and I'm the warden of Quincy Correctional Facility in New York State. Will the witnesses please remain silent and if possible please avoid any unnecessary movement. Are the witnesses for the condemned confirmed?"

A team member spoke from the observation room. "Yes, sir."

"Are the witnesses for the media confirmed?"

"Yes, sir."

"Are the witnesses for the state confirmed?"

Again, Virgil was given an affirmative response.

"All witnesses are present and confirmed. At this time we will proceed with the court-ordered execution of Isaiah Raynard Blackwood. Mr. Blackwood do you have a final statement you would like to make?"

"Yeah," Blackwood said clearly. "I sure do." Total silence fell over the room as he opened his mouth and began talking like a man who had nothing to lose.

"Everybody in here tonight is here for their own private reasons, including me. Some of y'all are here to say good-bye, and some of y'all wish I would just shut up and die. Miss Paula, Ben, Ellen, and Dannie, I'm sorry for your grief. I know how much you loved Terrie and Ari, and from the bottom of my heart, I wish it had never happened. Regardless of what I said at my trial, I carry a share of guilt for my death tonight. I lived my life in a manner that led me straight to this chair, and

I'm ready and willing to accept the punishment for this crime.

"But just like I sit here prepared to answer for my sins, every one of you are damn sure gonna be called on to answer for yours too. Because for certain members of the population there is no such thing as justice in America. The state counsels men like me for our so-called crimes against society, yet you're unable to counsel yourselves for the crimes you've committed against humanity. How long do you think America can live with a foot in two worlds? Riding the fence between the haves and the have-nots? Your courts don't even recognize me as a man! In the eyes of the law I'm a cross between a demon and an animal. But I tell you tonight that that's a lie. There's not a whole lotta difference between me and you. Yeah, you wear the suits and carry the briefcase, and I take what I want and exploit your weaknesses. But when I die to-night a piece of you is sure to die with me. It's been said that the killing of one man is really the killing of all mankind, and I believe that.

"My time here is up and I'm cool with it. Because I can die anywhere. Whether it's sitting here in this chair or stretched out on the street. If not tonight, then probably tomorrow. Life ain't about how long you live, it's about the way you live it. I ain't never asked for your mercy or begged the courts to spare my life. What we're about to do here has nothing to do with right or wrong, innocence or guilt. But since you've all gathered together in *my* name tonight, know that even so-called respectable men like you can learn something from a hard-core criminal like me. You don't get no cool points just for living with yourself in this world. You gotta be able to die with yourself too. And for real, the best test of character is not what you do when the world is watching. It's what you do when the only eyes watching are God's. So pump up the juice and let's take care of business. Warden? Let's get it started."

The silence in the room was deafening. Long moments passed and nobody moved. Finally, the team leader gave Virgil an elbow nudge, and the warden cleared his throat and began to read.

"From the Honorable Jeffrey Mulligan, New York. The superior court of Garrette County the State of New York vs. Isaiah Blackwood. The court having set the defendant Isaiah Raynard Blackwood on the 12th day of October to be executed by the Department of Corrections in such penal institution that may be designated by the said Department in accordance with the laws of New York during a time period beginning October 5th and ending on October 12th. The execution of Isaiah

Blackwood is considered ordered and adjudged by the state of New York. The order has directed us to serve a copy of this upon the commissioner of the Department of Corrections, the Warden of New York State's Quincy Correctional Facility, the Attorney General of the State of New York, the District Attorney, the defendant, and last known counsel of record for the defendant. Here on the 12th day of October 2007 signed Judge Henry Fobbes, Superior Court, Garrette County, New York, by the corrections commencing at midnight . . ."

And then Virgil spoke the most difficult words of his life.

"U.S. Marshal, we are ready."

In the observation room, the air was charged with tension. Gabriel had switched seats with his mother and now sat between her and Deborah, who held a tissue to her nose and was crying softly.

Several reporters were scribbling on their little white pads, and the witnesses for the victims were hugging and staring toward the death chamber with wide eyes.

A mask was placed over Isaiah's head and moments later the initial burst of electricity was applied. Blackwood shot forward, straining against the leather restraints as his nose ruptured. Blood sprayed from the left side of his face mask and completely saturated his shirt. He moaned as his fists clenched and unclenched, and a sizzling sound could be heard as droplets of blood fell from beneath his mask. Two minutes later the current was cut and Blackwood slumped back in the chair, motionless but still struggling to breathe. To the horror of the witnesses he moaned several times, then a second jolt snapped him upright again, and this time the electrode that was attached to his right leg began to smoke and the odor of burning flesh spread throughout the room, gagging the guards and alarming the witnesses.

Horrified coughs and murmuring voices rose in the observation room and Virgil sprang into action.

He stepped over to the wall and threw a manual switch, cutting the flow of electricity, but it was too late. The minute-long surge had been all but completed, except for a final few seconds that ticked slowly past.

A charred odor filled the air, and a low moan escaped from beneath Blackwood's mask. Trying to hide the misery on his face, Virgil turned to the prison doctor. "Check him."

"Can't," the pink-faced little man said, his nose twitching. "His body has to cool before he can be examined. We have to wait six minutes."

They waited in silence as Blackwood's chest rose and fell slowly. He appeared to take five or six deep breaths every minute, and by the time the team leader announced that six minutes had passed, more coughing and soft crying could be heard coming from the observation room. A reporter stood up and placed his forehead against the wall as he heaved, and another was doubled over and fanning the air with both hands.

Virgil's eyes were cold as he searched for Gabriel Blackwood across the room, and to his surprise the cries were coming from him. Gabriel's shoulders shook with grief as he held his mother in his arms and wept into her hair. Della Blackwood just sat there. Staring ahead at the mask-covered form strapped into the chair.

The doctor quietly examined the readings from the electrocardiogram and the heart monitor. He walked over to Blackwood and checked his body for a pulse. He pressed a stethoscope to both wrists and then to his neck, listening for long moments.

Then he turned to Virgil with a grim look on his face.

"The prisoner has expired. I hereby pronounce him dead."

With a hammer of remorse and outrage banging in his chest, Virgil turned on the tape recorder and announced. "At approximately 12:18 A.M. on the 12th day of October

2007, the court-ordered execution of Isaiah Raynard Blackwood was carried out in accordance with the laws of the state of New York. Will the team chief please close the drapes, and will the witnesses be escorted from the room and downstairs to exit the institution."

EPILOGUE

The weather had broken, and the freezing temperatures that had plagued the Northeast for weeks had dropped back down into the normal range. The flavor of autumn had been forever altered, though, and the brilliant orange, red, and rust-colored leaves that hadn't been weighted to the ground by ice had been burned by the early-season frost and hung wilted and soggy from near-naked trees.

Such was the sight that greeted Gabriel as he opened his eyes the morning after his brother's execution. The sun was blazing its warmth down on the earth, shrugging

231

off the heavy clouds of yesterday and shining with the promise of a new tomorrow.

Gabriel lay on his back with Michelle snuggled in the crook of his arm. Her hair was soft on his cheek and her breathing was even. His iPod had been triggered on by his alarm clock, and outside, strange voices could be heard above the silky vocals of Michael Franks.

With his hand gently pressed to her head, Gabriel slid his arm from beneath his wife's neck. Rolling over, he reached across his nightstand and parted the miniblinds at his window. He looked down with a frown. He saw news vans and camera crews pulling up. Reporters with microphones. A small group of them, beginning to gather outside his yard and along the grassy field adjacent to his house.

He took his time getting out of bed, and when he did, he parted the blinds again and gave a short, cordial wave to the half dozen members of the press down below. Moments later he stripped out of his pajama pants and stepped into a steam-filled shower and began his morning ritual.

There wasn't the slightest variation in his routine. He brushed his teeth, flossed, shaved, and clipped his fingernails. He had oiled his hair and dabbed on his two-hundred-dollar cologne by the time Michelle awoke, and he greeted her with a smile as she stepped into their dressing room with a look of confusion on her face.

"What's going on?" she asked, her hair pulled back and her makeup-free skin soft and clear. "Why are those reporters outside? I thought we were done with them after last night. Is all this because of your award ceremony this morning?"

"Yeah, it looks that way," Gabriel answered. "You know how they are. It's probably a real slow news day today. The ceremony has gotten pretty big over the years, though. I have a feeling this year is going to be the biggest."

Gabriel headed downstairs as Michelle showered, his grin gone, his face a studied mask. In the foyer, a large brown envelope had been slipped under his door. His name was centered on it, and almost every other inch of it was covered with crayon, drawings and scribble-scrabble created by a childish hand. The voices outside had gotten louder. Gabriel pulled the curtain back from the glass door and was surprised to see a red-faced reporter right up on his steps.

She waved some papers in the air and called out loudly, "A few of us received an envelope this morning, sir. Can you come outside and verify if any of this is true?"

Gabriel didn't answer. He let the curtain fall and carried the envelope down the hall and into his office. With steady fingers, he slit the top off with his letter opener and extracted the stack of papers that were inside.

He read the short note first, then skimmed the documents it had been clipped to. There were photocopies of everything. Airline tickets, gas receipts, restaurant and hotel bills. All with the dates and locations highlighted in bright-glow orange marker.

There were newspaper clippings too, grainy photos of smiling young children beside tearful pictures of their parents and loved ones clutching teddy bears and holding candles in front of sidewalk memorials. The dates of the clippings had been circled, and a carefully drawn time line that illustrated the parallel between his out-of-town trips and the brutal crimes in the papers was the last document in the stack.

It was all there. Had been there all the time, but nobody had bothered to look.

Gabriel fingered the short note and read it again.

"Now the whole world knows."

There was no signature on it, but none was necessary.

He got up from his desk and spread the window blinds and peeked outside again. The bloodsuckers were getting restless. Gabriel was just about to let the blinds fall closed when he saw a familiar figure standing apart from the others, leaning against a small white car. The brother was tall and intense. He wore a black leather coat and a leather apple jack on his head. His arms were folded as he stood quietly, staring toward the house. Gabriel chuckled, then sat back down and opened the bottom drawer of his desk and took out his gun. He checked the chamber and reset the safety, then slipped it into his front pants pocket.

Feeling the cool metal pressed to his leg, Gabriel glanced around his office, noting his fine possessions. It wasn't Gracie Mansion, but it was a hell of a long way from the projects. He sank back in the softness of his leather chair and closed his eyes, knowing that his dreams were about to come to an end. He'd gotten almost everything he'd wanted. Money. Prestige. Power. He'd hustled hard and achieved all of those things on his own. Not bad for a brother from the hood. But it had all been a lie. A smoke screen. A well-placed mask used to hide the sickness that had always driven him.

He scooted closer to his desk and reached for the acceptance speech he had prepared for the morning's ceremony. With his pen gripped firmly in his hand, Gabriel sighed, then leaned forward and began to make a few changes.

The annual awards given by the African-American Council for the Humanities were being held at the beautiful

235

Brooklyn Museum this year, and Gabriel and Michelle were swamped by reporters as they dashed the short distance from the side doorway of their home and into the car where Della was waiting with their hired driver.

"Don't listen to them and don't make any comments," Gabriel warned Della and Michelle before opening the door. Once outside, Gabriel waved and smiled at the reporters, but his wife and mother kept their heads lowered and their mouths closed. Their driver muttered under his breath as he maneuvered out of the driveway and down the street, doing his best not to hit anyone as they made their way out of the stately subdivision.

Less than an hour later they'd been whisked into the Brooklyn Museum and Gabriel was giving the security staff a few strict orders.

"Look," he told them, his voice smooth and his manner polished. "Nobody gets next to my family, okay? I mean it. I want the press a mile back. And no questions get thrown at me either, you understand? The first reporter who mouths off gets tossed out the door. Let the rest follow him if they don't get the point. I promise, all questions will have been answered by the end of the program. Tell them that."

Standing at the podium with Della and Michelle seated in the front row, Gabriel beamed under the spotlight as the crowd of supporters cheered and applauded. A representative of the Congressional Black Caucus was on hand to slip the ribbon around his neck, and when the noise died down and it was time for Gabriel to speak, he looked first at Michelle and then at Della.

"Thank you everyone who came here this morning for this celebratory occasion. I stand at the end of a long line of great people who've been bestowed with this honor, but unfortunately . . . I don't deserve it. By now you all know that my brother Isaiah was executed last night. He was murdered in cold blood, and every one of us here today had a hand in it. Over the years I've spoken out in support of my brother, but never once did I say that he was innocent of the crimes he was accused of committing. Yet the truth is, my brother Shyne, my identical twin, was no more guilty of killing Terrie and Arielle than any of you are.

"But something gets bent in a child's soul when it's trampled on too long. My brother Shyne got the short end of everything in life, and if he hadn't learned to take what he needed he would have been dead before we were ten because there was no one in his life, not even me, who ever gave him a damn thing.

"You all may not know this, but there were actually three of us. Triplets. Shadow, Shug, and Shyne. When we were six, our brother Shadow was killed. That's when it all changed. Mama almost died with Shadow, and Shyne and I swore we never wanted to see that kind of pain in our mother's eyes again.

"Shyne took the blame for killing Shadow . . . but I was the one who did it."

There was a collective intake of breath, then silence washed over the whole room. Gabriel raised his head and the spotlight illuminated his tears. He looked at Della and said quietly, "I don't know why I did it, but I did. I pushed Shadow out that window, Mama. It was me, not Shyne. Everything you ever blamed him for, it was me. Always *me*.

"Shyne took the heat for me. Every single time. It was easy for everybody to focus on Shyne. He was a criminal. A killer and a thief. But he was real. Yet nobody ever looked twice at me. And even if they did . . . I always had a solid alibi. My mother."

A tormented look washed over Gabriel as he leaned across the podium and stretched his trembling hands out to Della, his face contorted in pain.

"Why? *Why?* You loved me enough to lie for me, Mama? To close your eyes and act like you were blind? Didn't you know that was *too* much love? Way too much love? Why didn't you just tell the truth and put a stop to all this? Just one time? You could have saved Shyne's life last night, Mama, but instead you hated him enough to let me kill him."

A gasp rose in the air as Della cried out and pressed her hands to her mouth. Near the doorway, security guards were holding back a wave of newly arrived reporters who were grasping big brown envelopes and trying to push their way into the room.

Gabriel was out of time. More reporters had received their packets, and pretty soon his crimes would be all over the news. He saw that Virgil Banks had slipped inside and was staring at him like a dark conscience from the back of the room. Gabriel spoke quickly, his words coming out in a desperate rush.

"I'm sick, Mama. I've always been sick." Sweat dotted his temples and his body trembled. "I tried, but I could never help it." Gabriel cleared his throat and confessed loudly into the air. "I killed Terrie and Arielle Mills. It was me. Nobody but me.

"I know you've heard it said before that you should never judge a book by its cover. Well Shyne is dead, and I'm here to tell you today that you should never execute a criminal because of his brother!"

Gabriel reached into his front pants pocket and brought his gun to his temple.

"I'm sorry, Mama. Shadow's death started it all, and me and Shyne never wanted to see that kind of look in your eyes again. So please don't look at me, Mama. Turn your head. Please, Mama. Turn your head."

Michelle Blackwood screamed. She lunged toward her husband just as a bullet exploded from its chamber. She screamed again, and the room erupted in chaos as Gabriel Blackwood fell to the floor.

It was springtime in New York and Della Blackwood stepped out of the taxi onto a tree-lined path in Saintly Praise Cemetery with a large bouquet of flowers clutched in her hand.

She walked along the path until she came to a certain row and then sank her feet into the dew-moistened grass and walked down a ways. The grave she paused before was old but well tended. The stone had recently been cleaned and the engraving read EZEKIEL "SHADOW" BLACK-WOOD. Della plucked a single flower from the bunch and placed it near the headstone, then moved farther down until she found the spot where her other son lay. The grave was nicely shaded and almost completely covered in grass. The headstone had only recently been set.

She pulled half of the flowers from the bouquet and

carefully arranged them in a semicircle near the center of the mound. That done, she stood back and gazed down at the grave, shaking her head in sadness and remorse.

"You crazy-ass boy," she chastised lightly. "I was wrong about you. If only I hadn't been so blind and so stupid! You mighta been able to go far in life. Why'd you have to go and kill yourself over that fool?"

Della blinked back tears as waves of guilt swept over her. But what mother hadn't made some mistakes? How many could say they wouldn't go back and change a few things if they could? You couldn't help what got passed along in your blood, but Della alone was responsible for what had happened to her boys. In trying so hard to hold on to everything, she had lost everyone. And now she was alone with her memories and her grief. Alone with her conscience.

"I love you, my son," Della whispered and tossed all but one flower down onto the grave with the others.

The headstone read ISAIAH "SHYNE" BLACKWOOD 1970–2007.

With a last glance toward Shadow and final good-bye kiss blown to Shyne, Della moved down the row to leave the last flower for Shug.